The Lost Child

I0716612

Also by Leigh Swinbourne and published by Ginninderra Press

Novel
Shadow in the Forest

Stories
Away and other stories
The Shark and other stories

Leigh Swinbourne

The Lost Child
and other stories

The Lost Child and other stories
ISBN 978 1 76109 672 3
Copyright © text Leigh Swinbourne 2024
Cover: Cathy McAuliffe Design

First published 2024 by
GINNINDERRA PRESS
PO Box 3461 Port Adelaide 5015
www.ginninderrapress.com.au

Contents

The Lost Child 7

The Wild Horses 39

The Ultimate Economy 44

The Idol 52

The Sundowners 65

Final Role 102

Alana 112

My New Friend 120

The Lost Child

Ricky pulled over too quickly, wincing as his left front tyre bit into the gutter. He switched off the motor, which switched off the radio, and sat in a silence marked by the slow ticking of the engine and its lingering stink of petrol. Trying to put his head together. Stupid to feel anxious, rattled, nothing to be anxious about, simply the tail end of the speed. Hopefully by now he had almost worn the stuff out and could catch a couple of hours' kip after this last shift. Not if he was like this.

He had been up two nights, by design. When he found the envelope at the back of his socks drawer with the three little white pills, he immediately rang up the two different shift teams, one for disability, the other for aged care, and put in for the overnighters plus some day shifts before he could think the better of it. It was against the rules but it was unlikely the teams would cross-check. They were too flat out.

The pills were Jennie's but she was long gone, over a year now. He knew it would keep him going, and it was an inspiration too, a spur to earn much needed coin. It was just that at this point, predictably, he felt like a piece of shit. His mouth was dry, his underarms damp, his head buzzing and he was woozy in the gut. Still, after these final two hours, the weekend beckoned: rest and recuperation. He reached into his jacket pocket where, rooting amongst hardened balls of Kleenexes, he found a pellet of chewing gum which he popped in his mouth to work up some moisture. He had just driven from his unit two blocks away, briefly dropping in for a shower and two slices of toast and Vegemite that he had, with difficulty, washed down with half a can of flat Red Bull.

The clouds shifted and early afternoon autumn sunshine broke blessedly through the windscreen onto his face. He glanced at his reflection, hair thinning, already. Maybe he could use the money to replace the tyres which were now worn smooth. He'd surely be picked up sooner or later. The car hadn't had a service in ages, it was over-revving and the gear shift didn't feel right. But if he wanted to do all of that, he'd need to pop another little white pill. Maybe next week, or after.

Anyway, this would be a nice easy one to end the week: Gertrude Schmidt. He hadn't seen her for months – Jackie must be ill or something – a lovely lovely old soul. Hopefully her dementia was steady. The office file notes said it was still only mild, although they were probably out of date and realistically she would have gone downhill a bit. Invariably, after a cuppa and a chat, all Gertrude wanted to do was drive to Cornelian Bay and watch the river and bird life. Easy as. It was warm enough for that today, but she liked going there in the winter too, just to get out, he supposed.

He marked the commencement of the shift but sat a little longer. Gertrude's house was hidden by an odd fence constructed of bound saplings, presumably by the original owner. They built everything themselves in those days. Like the other houses in the street, it was a Federation – he was bringing it to mind – big junk-filled rooms with cobwebs looping from the ceilings, but like most of his clients she only lived in one, a spacious kitchen at the back. There she had everything she needed: stove, fridge, heater, a day-couch for sleeping and a Laminex table at which she could while away the hours studying her Lutheran Bible, all in her native German. She didn't like the television, said she was too old for it.

He shifted the gate aside, repositioned it – it was still broken – walked up the porch, rang the bell and called out her name. Nothing. He noticed that one of the panes in the left front room was held together with packing tape. He rang and called her again. She had to be home. He pushed up through the overgrown side path and looked in through the kitchen window. There she was, hunched over her Bible, miming the foreign vowels and gutturals. He rapped sharply. She looked up confused, then gave him a smile of recognition. He returned to the front, where she was waiting for him and she gave him a tight hug.

'Ricky, Ricky, how are you?' The warm frail body like a bird's. Tears welled in his eyes. She was squeezing them out.

'How are you, Gertrude?'

'Oh, all right, I suppose.' Her face focused as though she was reaching for a forgotten thread. 'I don't know. Come in.'

The place was an icebox. Stale dead air. At least in the kitchen they had the sun. The kitchen looked orderly – all the framed family photos and other knick-knacks Ricky recalled – but the garden through the back windows was an unruly tangle.

'Doesn't your son come and do the lawns?'

'He's moved to Melbourne. I don't know.'

They sat quietly over big chipped steaming mugs. The tea was strong, good, just what he needed. He checked her over quietly. Some time had passed, but still, her hair definitely looked thinner (what about his own?) and also she appeared to him just that little more shrunken into herself. Yes, she was gradually withdrawing, voluntarily, involuntarily, it was difficult to know.

'Another tea, Ricky?'

'Yeah, sure, thanks.'

But generally she seemed all right, probably in some ways better than him. He scanned the shift notes, Jackie's spidery handwriting. All pretty much as usual. The fridge had milk, eggs and meatloaf that she made herself. No vegetables, but there were lemons and bananas in a bowl on the table. Oats, bread. No strange smells. She was cleanly dressed, decently groomed.

'Gertrude, are you up for a walk at Cornelian Bay?'

'Yesterday a little girl died.'

'Sorry?'

'A little girl was hit by a car, in the front of my house.'

'Here?'

'She was killed.'

Ricky thought for a moment. Any accident like that would have been in *The Mercury*, the last few days' editions of which he'd read back to front and back again along with a heap of other crap, *New Idea*, *Women's Day*, through the long graveyard hours. Anyway, she couldn't see the road from the house.

'Are you sure?'

'A little girl. She was killed. She used to come and visit.'

He looked into Gertrude's pale blue eyes, her kindly creased face. 'What was her name?'

'I don't know. She used to come and visit.'

Some memory, or fantasy nightmare.

'Can you take me to Cornelian Bay today, Ricky?'

'Of course. We'll just finish our tea.'

'We walked in the garden together. Would you like some lemons? They're from my tree.'

'Sure. I'll take some.'

'Come.' Gertrude rose stiffly, reached for a plastic Woolworths bag, and opened the back door.

Ricky followed. The garden was terrible, wet grass knee high, windfall fruit covered in wasps. Next week, he'd contact the case officer, see if they could do something about it.

Gertrude methodically filled the bag with lemons.

'That's enough. Thanks.' He bent down and picked up a bright red, what did Jennie call them? Scrunchies. A bright red scrunchie buried in the grass. 'Here, you must have dropped this.'

'Not me, that little girl.' She took it from him and turned it over in her papery hand.

It did look like the type of hairband a girl would wear. Gertrude's thin white hair was always severely pulled back into a bun held in place by a tortoiseshell comb.

'So sad.'

'Gertrude, how did that front window break?' He already knew the answer.

'That's how I met her. It was an accident. She didn't mean it.'

'Thanks for these. Let's go down to the bay, shall we.'

'Yes. Cornelian Bay.'

The usual confusion with the house keys, then he eased her into the car. When he switched on the ignition, the rock music immediately blasted, affronting them both. He flicked it off.

'I'm sorry.'

'It's horrible, Ricky.'

'We'll go to the bay.'

Some staff couldn't cope with the dementia clients because of the conversations. When Gertrude talked, it was in large jagged pieces, with silent spaces between, and also smaller pieces, which over many shifts you fitted together to make up a series of pictures or parts thereof, something like the huge multi-piece jigsaws that his parents used to play with as kids that now only existed in the nursing homes Ricky had started out in. Of course, many of the pieces were missing. The trick to listening was to semi tune out, not concentrate or focus, and just let the fragments float around in your mind until you could join up a few. You didn't really need to respond, not precisely anyway, for the clients weren't so interested in actual conversing as reliving. And anyway what was most important to them, always, was the company. You simply had to be there for them. Company, and also a witness. Over time, and with the addition of a few biographical case notes, Ricky had pretty much assembled Gertrude's story.

Gertrude Schmidt had been born in 1931 in the Sudetenland in what was then Czechoslovakia. She was German, as was her entire community. Her father was the local schoolmaster and taught alone at the only school in the area, half an hour's walk from her village. It still amazed Ricky how with many dementia clients, the mind, perhaps in some bizarre compensation for losing its grasp on the present, brought back such incredibly detailed remembrances of the past. One memory sharpening as another faded.

And not just the past, but distant childhood. Ricky was twenty-five but there was no way he could recall his own childhood with the crystalline clarity that eighty-four-year-old Gertrude could and did. She had described to him time and again, in slightly variant versions, the long walk to the school through the starkly different seasons of the year – it was like a fairy tale for her – and also the various personalities of her family, neighbours and schoolfellows. All long lost to her.

When the Nazis invaded, life went on pretty much as usual, a few deprivations, but with the eventual defeat, the Czechs took their revenge. The German population that had lived there for centuries was savagely driven out. Gertrude's parents and the two girls came as penniless refugees into a camp in Bavaria. First her mother, then her father died of typhus. She was quarantined from her sister, became ill herself, then got well, then was sent to the other end of the world, to Hobart, as a DP, a displaced person.

Decades later, a settled married middle-aged woman with a working husband and two grown sons, she travelled alone back to her village which had been completely erased and built over. Not one building survived, not even the school or the old stone church. It was a Czech housing estate, a decaying communist relic. It would also be torn down shortly. The fairy tale childhood – the established traditions and community and little apple-cheeked Gertrude securely loved and cherished within it all – existed now only in her conversations with Ricky and the other carers.

In her long life, she had moved on from this of course, but now at the end, it seemed she couldn't leave it alone. The husband dead, both sons in Melbourne. Other than the three weekly visits from the carers, there was nothing to interrupt her mind brooding on what it would. Except for her Bible, which Ricky thought, was probably a further vehicle for brooding in a way, particularly considering the language. Alone with her Bible and her memories, Gertrude shifted into a parallel world. *Die Bibel*: a vast compendium of visions, holy men raving in the desert and elsewhere. What did they see and hear? What was he missing that Gertrude knew?

He parked the car, carefully, and the two of them sat looking out at the calm river. It was a popular scenic spot. To the left, the long bushy headland embracing the Cornelian Bay Cemetery that still served Hobart; to the right, the sweep of the bay past bright boxy boatsheds up to the Tasman Bridge elegantly spanning the Derwent. There was a layer of mist hanging over the water. Sign of cold weather on the way.

'Do you want to go for a walk?'

'A walk. Yes.'

He helped her from the car. She had a walking stick, her left leg was stiffer than her right, but despite her limp she set off at a determined pace towards the boatsheds.

He grabbed his jacket from the back seat, locked the car and caught her up. 'It's sunny now. A nice day,' he said.

She didn't respond; perhaps she didn't hear. And in fact, one of the things Ricky really liked about old people (thinking back to the conversations) was that they never showed any particular interest in him, what he was doing, what he was going to do, all of which presently didn't bear much scrutiny. Post-school, he had moved out of home and embarked on a science degree at Tas Uni with genuine enthusiasm, but then had dropped out after only a year and a half. The courses were interesting and the teaching fine but for some reason he had lost motivation. Then there were various jobs and now this one, casual aged and disability carer. A job without much pressure and no expectations, unless he wanted to create them. His present life had no direction or purpose, which was why Jennie had finally returned to Perth, leaving in her wake a mild melancholy that he hadn't managed to slough off.

'You're still a child, Ricky.' Touching his cheek tenderly as she left.

He had never been to Perth, imagined it full of sunshine and vitality, a sort of fantasy Australia that the Brits might conjure from *Home and Away* or *Neighbours*. He hadn't had a girlfriend since Jennie, hadn't had sex, save for the hand-held kind. All this worried him, but not sufficiently to do anything about it. He needed to go back and finish his degree. He intended to, but he just never seemed to get around to it.

Truth was, he could do this job forever. He liked it, but the low pay meant he would never be able to afford a home, or a family. He didn't have a great deal in common with his work colleagues, who he never saw much of anyway. Almost all of them had working-class backgrounds and lived in the northern suburbs, and they all seemed to know one another. It was a female-heavy workplace, but most of the women were middle-aged plus and many of them were gay. Back when he was with Jennie, he had made a bit of an effort, kept up, got together with old mates and their partners for drinks and films. After she left, all his school and uni friends seemed to drop away. Nobody rang him because he didn't ring. Except for occasional dinners at the family home across the river at Lindisfarne (where he endured the rote family criticisms), he was now basically living an isolated life. Just like his clients.

Gertrude was heading for an aluminium bench. She sat with a sigh. Her blue eyes scanned the bay. 'It is very still,' she said.

It was. The wind had dropped, the sun shone, Cornelian Bay was picture postcard. Ricky needed to piss. The speed still – he'd pissed not long ago at home.

He looked around and spied a toilet block further up the hill behind the boatsheds. 'Gertrude, I need to go to the toilet. Will you be all right here?'

'Yes, you go. I'll sit.'

She'd be fine. What could happen? She couldn't move quickly enough for him to lose her. He hiked up towards the block. It looked fresh and bright but inside was full of filth and graffiti. He went behind it into some bushes and emptied his bladder of virtually nothing.

When he walked around the front and looked for Gertrude, she had left the bench. He spotted her at a considerable distance down on the beach. He couldn't see her clearly. He was looking into the sun. She was bent talking to someone, a kid. There was an enclosed playground nearby jumping with kids, their shrieks and cries mingled with those of the gulls. He jogged down. When he reached Gertrude, she was alone. The 'beach', hard river mud, stank of low tide, natural but nauseous.

'You were talking to one of the children.'

'No, no, only the birds. We bring some bread next time.' She was smiling at a family of ducks.

'I thought I saw you talking to a child.'

'Think how happy they must feel, Ricky, flying over the waters.'

It must have been a trick of the light. It was because she'd talked about that child earlier. He was becoming crazy as his clients. God, he felt wrung out.

'I want to go to the graveyard.' She had never asked this before.

'Sure. Do you want to walk or drive up there?'

'I don't know. We can walk. Ricky, I want to try and find that little girl's grave.'

'But you don't know her name.'

'Her name was Sophie.'

'Sophie.'

'That's right. Let's go.'

Might as well humour her. She'd probably tire out before they reached the graveyard.

She set off with her determined limp in the opposite direction onto the path leading up around the headland. Ricky strolled beside her, hands clenched in his jeans' front pockets. Even with the gum, his mouth seemed foul. His head was throbbing and he wanted to lie down.

'Sophie had a message for me.'

'What was it?'

'I can't tell you.'

'You don't remember?'

'No, I can't tell you.'

The path rose but Gertrude climbed steadily with the incline. To their right were the waters of the bay, pleasure boats idle; to their left, the forest, cool and beneficent. Ricky inhaled the resin of the gums. At times, it was as if a gauze curtain had interposed itself between him and the world. Then, suddenly, he would feel incredibly raw, exposed; a bird call or a sharp reflection off the water piercing his brain. He only had to hack it another hour or so. Eventually, the path levelled out, the bush receded, and they walked into the outskirts of the graveyard.

Gertrude started up the nearest row, leaning forward and reading all the graves, one after another.

'Do you have any idea where she might be, Gertrude?'

'No.'

The site was extensive. Did she have a plan? Did it matter?

'Do you mind if I have a little rest while you look at the graves?'

'Of course not.'

'You promise you won't leave the graveyard without me or if you find what you're looking for, you'll come and get me.'

'I won't leave without you, Ricky.'

'Good.'

She continued, head bent, and he lay down gratefully beside a tomb on the cool dry dirt with the beetles and ants. God's fellow creatures. As soon as Ricky closed his eyes, he saw a little girl talking to Gertrude in her tangled backyard. She had a child's serious face and was telling something she needed to tell. He strained to understand the words but couldn't. She was ringing her hands together with the gravity of what she was saying. At some point, she impulsively reached behind her head, pulled off a bright red scrunchie and shook out her hair. As she talked on, he saw her negligently drop it into the long grass.

He woke. He was cold, shivering. How long had he been asleep? He staggered upright, brushed himself down, looked around for Gertrude but couldn't see her anywhere. He started up the row she had gone. Where was she? There were infinite rows. It was a nightmare. Each time he looked up one, he thought he caught sight of a small figure at the end of it, but when he focused, there was nothing.

Someone tapped him on the shoulder, scaring him half out of his wits. He spun around. It was Gertrude.

'Come, Ricky. I have found it.'

She led him to a fresh grave of a young girl. Some awful tragedy. Emily Nettlefold, aged seven.

'You said her name was Sophie.'

'No, Emily. Her name was Emily. This is her.'

'Her name was Sophie. Sophia Schmidt, the younger sister. Gertrude was devoted to her and the separation in the camp and eventual loss was a considerable trauma. Post-war, when she got on her feet here as a young woman, she tried to locate her, and made repeated attempts down the years, but couldn't find anything. Other than presumably an entry on an old birth registry filed away somewhere in the Czech Republic, there's nothing left of Sophia Schmidt.'

This was Jackie Cooper, Gertrude's usual carer. Ricky had dropped into the office Monday morning to collect a forgotten ten dollars due him in lieu of parking costs for the last staff meeting and caught her walking up the stairs. He'd wanted to mention the garden to her. She'd already spoken to the case officer and a detail was turning up this coming weekend.

'But there seems to be some other little girl. She talked about various conversations and told me she broke one of the front windows.'

'I taped that up. I don't know who broke it but it could have been anybody. My guess is a stray stone thrown from the street. There's a primary school down the end of the road and kids walk pass the house all the time.'

'I found a scrunchie in the backyard.'

'A what?'

'It's an elastic band girls wear in their hair these days. My last girl-friend used them.'

'There's all kind of junk in that backyard. Listen, Ricky, Gertrude's not as together as she seems. She mixes up times and people.'

'I don't know. She sounded pretty definite about this girl. She thought she'd been killed in a car accident outside the house.'

'Someone killed like that, it would have been in the news.'

'I know. I just felt there was something there. I mean, other than this sister.'

'Well, you can quiz her again this Friday. I've got a doctor's appointment.'

Jackie towered over Ricky on the stairs. On level ground, she stood six foot in her industrial boots, which she wore with blue denim overalls and flannelette shirts, summer and winter. Her grey hair was cropped close, she had a square handsome sun-browned face with two deep perpendicular lines etched in her cheeks. Once, cleaning out a house with her on a shift, sleeves rolled up, Ricky had seen a faded tattoo of an anchor, like a cartoon sailor's, on her left toned bicep. Jackie had been with the same partner for twenty years, Rowena, who also worked for Care Service Tasmania. All her clients were women, all her friends were women, she moved in a world of women: a gynaverse or something. Nevertheless, her relations with Ricky, with whom she shared a number of clients, were always friendly and cordial, even though, he imagined, she saw him as a separate species. Still, he considered, in her work all kinds of disabilities were a commonplace, so what was a mere penis after all.

'Incidentally, while I was getting myself a coffee earlier, I overheard some rosterers gossiping that you put in for two consecutive overnighters last week. I'm sure they wouldn't report it without telling you but I wouldn't make a habit of it.'

'I won't. Thanks.'

Driving from the office to his next shift, suddenly behind him was the fatal siren. Shit! He realised he'd just drifted through a temporary forty zone in sixty, some worksite typically with no workmen present. His mind had been elsewhere, now he was fucked. He pulled over and sat awaiting sentence. This was just what he needed.

'Morning, sir. Can I see your licence? You know you were doing sixty back there.'

'Sorry, officer, I didn't really notice the signs. I'm used to it as a sixty zone.'

There was an incredibly strained silence while the man examined his licence as though he were a terrorist, and then an inspection of his car. Great!

'Your tyres are bald. This vehicle shouldn't be on the road.'

He looked at the cop, who surprisingly had a genial friendly face. Forties, bit of flab, balding, like himself (how could he be balding in his mid-twenties?). He thought he'd seen him somewhere.

'Richard Slater. You used to drive the maxi-taxis, didn't you.'

Now Ricky remembered. Mrs Cummings. This was her son. He used to regularly pick her up from a nursing home at Sandy Bay and take her to his house in Lutana.

'Mrs Cummings. How's she doing?'

'She passed last year. You were very good to my mother.'

Christ Almighty! He was going to let him off. One lucky break.

'I'll give you a life, Richard, because of Mum. But get this shit-heap attended to, pronto.'

'Ricky. Thanks a million. I'm sorry, I've forgotten your name.'

'Joe, Joe Cummings. I'm just on traffic patrol this week as a fill-in. I work at the Bellerive station if you need anything.'

'Okay, thanks again. I'll get the car sorted, I promise you.'

'There won't be a next time.'

'Sure. See you later, Joe.'

'Take care.'

He drove off carefully. What would the tyres cost him? Five, six hundred bucks. He had to get it done now. Try on another double over-nighter. Bugger. Still, bloody lucky. Joe Cummings. A decent cop, good to know they were around.

It was Friday and Ricky was again sitting in his car outside Gertrude's in much the same state as the previous week. When he'd rung up the rostering team, he lucked on two consecutive newbies – such a stressed job there was always a high turnover – and with the help of pill number two, he'd done the overnighters again, one in disability and one in aged. They'd find him out, but last week they didn't even bother speaking to him, so surely he had a life here, like with Constable Cummings. But again he felt terrible. This would definitely be the last time. No warm sun through the windscreen. It was raining solidly. Cornelian Bay was out. Cups of tea and a mildly disorientating dementia conversation. That was okay. He also wanted to check out the backyard before the garden crew moved in tomorrow to see whether he could find any other objects like the scrunchie.

He didn't bother with the front door, just went up the side, drenching himself on the foliage, and tapped on the window. It was great she had the Bible. Most of his clients spent their lives in front of free-to-air television. One more example of technical advance eroding lifestyle. Did the type of community that Gertrude had known as a child exist anywhere in the world these days? He doubted it. Third world countries still had the sense of family and community, but the life there was poor both in material and medical terms; whereas life in the West now seemed completely dominated by multifarious gadgets that had largely replaced actual living.

The house was freezing again, and damp to boot. Gertrude hadn't bothered to turn the heat pump on. She probably didn't notice the cold. He found the remote under her shift notes and the machine wheezed reluctantly to life. Smelt like it hadn't been used in a while.

'Gertrude, you should keep yourself warm.'

'I forget, Ricky. I forget many things.' She paused. 'But death has forgotten me.' She gave a thin-lipped smile at this witticism which Ricky had heard many times.

'Too wet to go out today, but what about a cup of tea and a chat?'

'That would be nice.'

They talked in large loose loops. Ricky couldn't get into the rhythm of it and started to get a headache.

'Gertrude, do you mind if I go outside to clear my mind?'

'It's raining.'

'That doesn't matter.'

He stepped out the back into the wet grass and chill air, took a few damp deep oxygen-rich breaths. The rain had lightened to a drifting mist. He looked behind through the window and saw that Gertrude had returned to the Bible, her default existence. Ricky started at one end of the yard and systematically worked slowly up and down and across, like he was mowing. Near the base of a rotted pear tree, he found a second red scrunchie. As he fingered it, the rain came down again. He was almost done. He glanced up towards the final corner and spied a spot of colour amongst some particularly dense weeds. He squelched over, squatted down and dug out a pink mobile phone, wiped it clean in the rain. On the back in silver glitter-stick running diagonally were the letters E, gap, I, L, Y.

He stood there getting drenched. So Emily Nettlefold had been here. There were two little girls, even if Anna confused them occasionally. But when had she been here? Was the car accident sometime in the past? Did it matter? Probably not, other than proving a point with Jackie Cooper. He brought his findings back to Gertrude.

She turned the phone over in her hands. '*Ja*, she lost her phone. I remember.'

'When did you used to see her?'

'I don't know.'

'Why did she come here?'

'She was safe with me, Ricky. She could tell me things.'

'What things?'

'I promised not to tell.'

'Do you remember?'

'Some things. *Ja*. Not good.'

'But she's dead, Gertrude.'

'I promised, Ricky.'

And since she was dead, it didn't matter anyway. Why was he pursuing this? It could only confuse or distress Gertrude. He might as well drop the subject. He pocketed the phone.

'Another tea?'

'That would be nice.'

They sipped in companionable silence.

'Willow Court!' Gertrude suddenly exclaimed.

'Willow Court? What about Willow Court?'

'Dat is vat dis girl vas scared ov: Villow Court.' Gertrude had sunken into her German accent. She spoke softly, as to herself, without looking at Ricky. She was not certain about sharing this confidence. Then she looked directly at him. 'What is this place? Willow Court.'

'It's an old asylum, out at New Norfolk. It's been closed down for years. There was no way your Emily would have been old enough to have gone there.'

'That is the place she said. Other things, I can't tell you.'

'It's okay, Gertrude. Let's forget it.'

He heard his own phone ping. Since he only ever used it for work, he assumed the message probably concerned the overnighters. He'd been sprung. Enjoy the tea and quiet.

But when the shift was over and he accessed his messages, it was simply a note that his annual police check was due for renewal. Four o'clock. Newtown Police Station was just up on Main Road. Might as well get the thing done sooner rather than later.

The station waiting room was definitely colder than the outside air. Ricky sat there suffering with two other innocent paranoids. Why? Keep them all on edge, one of their many tactics. He idly scanned a chart of missing persons on the wall to his left and there it was: Emily Nettle-fold. Must be out of date, what with the grave. The photo was fuzzy, not clear – a generic nine- or ten-year-old with short bobbed hair – you couldn't really use it for identification.

He filled out his form in front of the bored officer, paid the fee, and then said, as he had not intended to, 'I might have some information on one of your missing persons, although she's dead now.'

The jowly old fellow sprung to life. 'How do you know she's dead?'

Ricky briefly told him about Gertrude and the grave.

'Take a seat, sir. I'll pass on your information.'

He waited and then a younger man appeared and ushered him into an office. He was tense and lean, like a greyhound, close-shaven cheeks shiny blue-black.

He leaned forward over his desk and eyeballed Ricky. 'I'm Inspector Cade. Tell me what you know about this girl.

Ricky repeated his story, ending with… 'but she's dead, officer.'

'She's not dead, Mr Slater. She's still missing.'

'What about the grave?'

'It's empty. After the girl had been gone for a year, her mother wanted closure and paid for a service and burial. On our books, she's still very much a missing person.'

'Only after a year? Seems odd.'

'The mother is a drug abuser and unstable. The loss of her child was too much, I guess, and this was a way of putting it behind her. She's a local, well known to us. I dealt with this case. The girl vanished and there were no leads at all. I need to speak to this client of yours.'

'Gertrude? She's just at her home, not far from here. You could drop in anytime. She has got dementia,though, and mixes this girl up with her little sister from her childhood in Europe. She did seem to think Emily had been hit by a car. I don't know if that's any help.'

'Maybe. If I could have your details and her address.'

'I'll give you mine, but you'll need to go through my work to get her details. I'm sure it won't be an issue.'

Sometime after Ricky arrived home, he realised he still had the girl's phone in his coat pocket. Maybe he should go back and hand it over to Cade, but it was now dark and raining again. Also he was comfortable and had drunk most of a bottle of wine and would be over the limit. Cade had probably gone home too. He'd call in next week when he was back in the area. Willow Court. Why would the girl mention that?

Ricky had never had occasion to visit the site of Willow Court up in the riverside town of New Norfolk, but he knew a fair bit anecdotally and otherwise about the institution and its background from his work with Care Service Tasmania. He dug his laptop out from underneath an empty pizza carton and googled the Wikipedia entry.

The Royal Derwent Hospital (Willow Court) was built to house mentally ill and mentally handicapped persons in 1827, soon after the separation of Van Diemen's Land from New South Wales. It was open for more than 170 years, finally closing in November 2000… Today parts of the hospital site are currently sitting derelict and it has been the subject of a great deal of vandalism… Willow Court has become notorious for supposed hauntings and ghost sightings…so much so that in February 2011 the Derwent Valley Council agreed to a paranormal investigation… There is no evidence of such haunting claims that have been verified by science.

Scenic New Norfolk, thirty minutes drive north of Hobart, seemingly now an unlikely place for such a notoriously dark extended episode in the state's history. For as Ricky knew from many of his clients, basically anyone who presented a social problem could potentially have been incarcerated at Willow Court: orphaned and unwanted children, lunatics, invalids, alcoholics, difficult teenagers, petty thieves; many of CST's clients had grown up there and some had been traumatised by their experiences: rapes, beatings, neglect, neglect above all.

Now, as Wikipedia detailed, the various buildings lay abandoned, and vagrants and drug addicts camped out in them. In fact, outcasts seemed peculiarly drawn to the place. It held a spell. Ricky switched off his computer and sat there with the last of the bottle considering how there are always certain people attracted to suffering and death, mostly damaged people, obviously, attempting catharsis, attempting justification, or simply moving in a world to which they were accustomed; but others too, drawn to what they thought was the edge of something. The rumours of hauntings, fuelled by various horror tales, still persisted in the broader community. He'd heard plenty. But still, all this was pretty old stuff. What could any of it have to do with a little girl living in Hobart? Maybe she had decamped out there for some reason. But then she'd told Gertrude she was scared of the place. Tales from her mother more like. Nightmares passed on down the line.

Tuesday morning, he was having a coffee between shifts when his phone rang.

'Ricky? This is Susan Long, Gertrude Schmidt's case officer. I have some bad news. Can you take this call now?'

Oh no, he hated this. Gertrude had had a fall or a stroke, or even worse.

He steeled himself. 'Yeah, tell me, Susan.'

'Gertrude's dead. She was found drowned in her bath yesterday by Jackie Cooper. She must have had a stroke or something and been unable to get out. Her sons have been informed and are flying in from Melbourne to organise the funeral and other details. Do you want to attend the funeral?'

'Yes, sure. God! I'm so sorry. It's weird she was in the bath, though. She only ever took showers because she was worried she didn't have the strength to pull herself out of the bath.'

'Maybe that's part of what happened. Ricky, do you need any assistance to deal with this?'

'No, I should be right. If it's worrying me, interfering with work, I'll give you a call, I promise. I've only one more shift today. Thanks, Susan.'

He lingered in the café, down and listless. His phone rang again. He had to come in and see the boss, Jeremy Cousins, about the overnighters. What a day. He roused himself for his next shift, and when it was done, drove to the office in town.

He sat quiet and attentive while a pacing Jeremy Cousins bawled him out good and proper. This was okay. If Cousins was bawling him out, he wasn't going to sack him. It would go on his record but he'd just be a good boy from now on. He tried to look contrite, but he was hacking this tirade with little response because his mind was still on Gertrude. Aside from the tragedy of her death, there was this business about the bath that was bugging him. He'd never known her to take a bath. He must talk to Jackie about it, if she was up to it. Imagine finding her. Still, these things happened. He'd been lucky so far. He'd lost clients but none on his watch.

'Have you nothing to say for yourself?'

Jeremy Cousins was straight from the copybook of overweight, over-stressed, underpaid, forty-plus petty executives, forever copping it from above and copping it from below. The only thing distinctive about him was his high piping voice. He reminded Ricky of a bun-eating boy chorister, and had probably been one. This was all a bit of a charade, Cousins wasn't a natural tyrant, which is why he was where he was and no higher. It was a difficult lousy job and Ricky didn't envy him.

'I promise you, Mr Cousins it, won't happen again. I just really needed the money. I was stupid. I see that now.'

'We have a duty of care to these vulnerable people. You need to be fully on the ball for them, Richard. That's why the rule is there.'

'I understand that. I realise I've made a mistake. I'm sorry. As I said, it won't happen again, believe me.'

'It won't, or you'll be out the door, son.'

He was certainly pleased to walk out Cousins's door. Instead of chasing up Jackie, she was there waiting for him downstairs in the foyer.

'I've had to write a report on Gertrude. Someone told me you were with Jeremy, so I thought I'd see how you were taking it.'

'You mean Gertrude, not Cousins.'

'Of course.'

'Well, how are you taking it? I mean, Jesus, Jackie, you're the one who found her.'

'Very sad. It's not the first time for me.'

'Listen, Jackie, Gertrude never had a bath. She always had a shower. You know that. She thought she couldn't get out of the bath.'

'She couldn't, Ricky, that's why she drowned.'

'But what was she doing there in the first place?'

'She had dementia. Maybe she forgot she couldn't get out of the bath. I don't know. What's your point?'

'I think it's a bit suspicious.'

'What? What are you saying? That somebody drowned Gertrude? Who? Why? Ricky, she died in an accident. Accept it.'

'Well, I still think it's weird.'

'Look, nobody saw her from day to day except us. An innocent harmless old woman. I was there, remember. There was no sign of forced entry, nothing was stolen or anything. There wasn't anything of value in the place anyway, not even a television. The cops and ambos found nothing suspicious. Why would anyone want to kill Gertrude Schmidt?'

'Maybe because she knew something.'

'Knew what?'

'I don't know. Something Emily Nettlefold told her.'

'There is no Emily Nettlefold, not in Gertrude's life anyway. It was just a grave she happened upon. All the little girl stuff is her sister. We've been through this.'

'There was an Emily Nettlefold, actually. I found that out. She's a missing person. And I think Emily Nettlefold knew something that she shouldn't have known for some reason, and she told Gertrude and then there was a possible risk Gertrude would tell someone like me or you.'

'But she didn't, did she? Whatever her relationship with this girl, Gertrude didn't tell me anything, and she didn't tell you anything. I want you to be rational here.'

'I don't know. Maybe she did. Maybe in all that endless talk there's something we didn't pick up on.'

'Ricky, this is crazy. Are you trying to make yourself believe this or something? Okay, you cannot accept she died, accidentally, by her own hand. I guess I can understand that, you were fond of her. I was too, God knows, but if you start going on in this way, you'll upset the family and also put your job in jeopardy, if it's not that way already.'

'The family? Two sons who ignored her.'

'All right, fuck the family, but I'm right about your job, eh? Look, you're a good carer, don't stuff yourself up because someone you were attached to died. People die in this job. You know that. It's happened before, it will happen again. If you really have serious doubts about all this business with the girl and with Gertrude, something you think's not being noticed, then take it to the police. They're the professionals. Let them judge and deal with it.'

'You sure no one saw her regularly besides you and me?'

'Listen, Ricky, just leave it alone, please.'

There was an intruder in the house. Terror possessed him, he had to get out. Too late, they were upon him, they were too strong, a hand over his mouth, he couldn't escape or cry out, now they were pushing him down, down into the dark, he was suffocating, he was going to die… He woke up sweat-soaked with a Bundy and coke still gripped in his hand. Jesus! How much had he drunk? What time was it? He checked his phone. Three-thirty. Shit! When was his first shift? Eleven. He still had some time for sleep. He staggered into the kitchen and boiled up an instant coffee, then slumped back onto the couch.

Ricky sat there, sipping the scalding drink, trying to think logically through it all. He knew he had a tendency to paranoia, and any ingesting of speed accentuated it, but still, there were definitely a few worrying factors. Like the sequence of events. He told Inspector Cade about Emily and then Gertrude died. It was a very big stretch, but what if those two things were somehow linked? If Gertrude really had been killed, and telling Cade had triggered that off, it meant either that Cade was corrupt or he had informed someone else who was corrupt. Cade had told someone about Gertrude and Emily who then killed Gertrude rather than concerning himself about what she might or might not know, or perhaps before Cade could find that out. Killing Gertrude and making it appear an accident was relatively easy. She was a loose cannon, what with the carers and all, blabbing about. Maybe he shouldn't go back to Cade with Emily's phone. Or just yet anyway.

He brought to mind an old uni drinking/smoking mate, Trevor Holsworthy, a tech nut. Trev had been a brilliant computer science student but dropped out before finishing his degree like Ricky. Ricky hadn't spoken to him in years but knew that he worked at JB Hi-Fi in the city. When he went to the store occasionally, he always saw him behind the computer desk. Perhaps Trev could tell him something from Emily's phone. What could he give Trev for the favour? The last speed tablet. He knew Trev would go for that and Ricky had road tested the pills already.

Next day, he'd finished by four thirty; he drove into town and chased up Trev, who agreed to a drink after closing. Over multiple schooners, Ricky told him the whole story of Gertrude, which he was thinking while he was doing it was probably not such a bright idea, but he was now bursting for a sympathetic hearing and he knew he could trust Trev, if only for the reason that Ricky considered him to be one of the most unworldly souls he had ever known. Bordering on obese, with bottle-lensed glasses and a wild brown afro that now, amazingly, was turning grey, the man was a true original. Ricky had never known him to have a girlfriend; an only child, he lived with his invalid father and whacky mother who never left their house. Beneath which was an extensive makeshift basement that Ricky had regularly visited back in student days for marathon weed sessions, Trev's den, crammed end-to-end floor-to-ceiling with electronic junk. If anyone could crack Emily's phone, Trev could.

'This speed okay?'

'I've done two pills myself. Parting gift of a girlfriend.'

'I'll give it a good go, Ricky, but no promises. You give me the speed regardless.'

'No worries. You'll get it when you're done.'

So that was that. What next? Cade appeared straight, but then what did Ricky know? What about Joe Cummings? There were a couple of favours swapped here already, a proto-personal relationship. Maybe Cummings could have a look at the Emily Nettlefold case, probably discreetly, presumably it wasn't really his business, but still, he was a copper, he was on the inside. The Hobart police force couldn't be all that big, they must pretty much know one another's turf, or be able to find out about it. Ricky could tell Joe Cummings about his concerns. Then Cummings could check out Cade for Ricky, and establish whether he was on the level. Then Ricky could approach Cade with whatever he found out from Trev, and justice could be done for Gertrude and perhaps Emily too. But he'd have to get his tyres replaced first. And he'd have to wait at least a couple of pays to do that. Still, that was a plan: fix the car, then see Cummings.

Then it happened again. Ricky was reaching for some clean socks, or not very dirty ones, right at the back of his drawer and, presto, another envelope. Six little pills this time, a real bonanza. What had Jennie been up to? Could he perhaps sell them and get the money to fix the car? It didn't sound a smart idea; he didn't know any drug dealers and was sure to be ripped off and maybe get himself into strife. He could do the double shift thing one more time. He was sure Jeremy Cousins wouldn't sack him, just dress him down again – that is, if he was caught. He figured he was just unlucky the last time, and the time before that.

Ricky gave it a week, took a pill, did a day-night-day, and nothing happened. So he did it again. He got sufficient in his subsequent pay to replace his tyres, and then rang up the Bellerive police and made an appointment on his next free afternoon to see Joe Cummings.

Except a week or so later when he drove over the river to the Bellerive Police Station, he found himself eyeball-to-eyeball with Inspector Cade.

'Officer Cummings has been transferred up north. What did you want to see him about?'

'He asked me to report back to him when I got my car fixed up,' Ricky lied. How did Wade even know he was seeing Cummings?

'Let's not worry about your car. You got anything further to tell me about the Nettlefold girl or this client of yours?'

'Gertrude Schmidt has died.'

'I know. Go home, Ricky.'

Driving back over the bridge, Ricky felt unnerved. Gertrude, Emily, Wade: there was something they all knew that he didn't, something crucial, that told whether Gertrude was murdered and if so what for and also what happened to the girl. Was she a mule for these men? Or worse, was the mother pimping her out for her fixes? Or both. He realised yet again he'd forgotten the mobile, also the mention of Willow Court. Not to worry. He'd see if Trev came up with anything and then pass the phone and info onto Cade, and then try and forget about it all.

Saturday morning, Ricky was vainly trying to sleep in, twitching in sour sheets, when his phone pinged and it was Trev.

'Done what I can, mate. Not much. Do you want to meet somewhere?'

'I'll come to you.'

Ricky took a salutary swig from the Bundy beside his bed, dressed and drove straight over. Trev's family home was in the northern working-class suburb of Chigwell; as far as Ricky knew, Trev's parents had lived in this rented decaying unpainted weatherboard their entire married lives. The front yard was wildly overgrown and littered with stripped-down husks of cars and their rusted entrails, plastic sheeting, lengths of rope, lengths of timber, crates of empty beer stubbies, odd bits of piping, a toilet, a bath and, secreted in the long grass, multiple dog turds from the two glossy black Labradors that escorted Ricky to the front door. The door was unlocked which was just as well as there was no way Trev's mum, Gloria, could have heard him knock over the sound of the television.

'I'm Ricky, an old friend of Trev's.'

'What, luv?'

Gloria was clad in an oversize purple muumuu, maybe to disguise her weight. Ricky recognised the puffy face and unkempt curly grey hair, older now. Smelling as if she hadn't washed for a while.

'A FRIEND OF TREVOR'S.'

'Come in and I'll make you a cuppa. He's downstairs.'

Ricky followed her into the living room, dominated by the glossy wide screen like an angry god. Trev's father, Reg, was dozing on a cracked leather two-seater, looking like a true-blue battler, which is what he was. A still powerful body, chesty with short legs, a face skull-like now with age and glowing surreally in the flickering light from the telly, no hair, dentures slipping, line of drool.

'HELLO, MR HOLSWORTHY.'

No response. The television shouted at him, at them all. There were the ads, even louder, regularly interrupting the shows, repeating themselves, that paid for the shows. Then there were the shows, mostly made up of longer ads, product placement and 'scientific' information about the products, that also paid for the shows. The shows must go on, and on. Skin restorers, hair restorers, miracle mattresses, dodgy nutritional supplements… Who bought all this? Somebody obviously. But not Trev's mother, who had surely long given up on the fountain of youth.

Trev appeared. 'Hi, Ricky. Mum, can we turn down the telly?'

'Your father's lost the remote.'

'How did you turn it on?'

'At the power switch.'

'Can I turn it off?'

'Why?'

'You're not watching it.'

'It gives your dad company.'

'Dad's asleep.'

'If you turn it off, it'll wake him up.'

Shouted at the top of their voices, like they were all in a nightclub. Trev's mum went into the kitchen. Trev followed the power cord and flicked off the switch. The silence rang.

His father woke up. 'G'day, son. A pound for a pound. A dozen skins made up a pound. One night, we shot one-hundred-and-forty-four. I'd skin 'em and Joey'd gut 'em. Out in the chook shed. Regular factory. Good money in winter. Couldn't have survived on just my wage. Twelve pennies a week.'

Ricky now remembered that Reg had frontal lobe damage caused by a rare disease, cyptococcal, which he had caught from the tons of droppings from pigeons he had bred and raced throughout his life. He had two obsessions: rabbit shooting and the number twelve, which was related to his conviction that the country should never have changed from imperial to decimal currency in 1966. Reg's 'conversation' was much like the ads.

'A pound for a pound. A dozen skins...'

Trev went into the kitchen after his mother and Ricky followed. The sink was full of mugs and dishes; on the neighbouring benches were pizza cartons, Webster packs, soiled ashtrays and empty dog food tins. A recycling bin was full of stubbies. Bulging garbage bags leaned against the far wall. These were surmounted by an extensive assortment of battered aluminium saucepans themselves surmounted by cereal boxes and rolls of toilet paper. From out of this chaos, Gloria handed them both a cup of tea. They all shifted back into the living room and Gloria turned on the television. This did not send Reg back to sleep but it did stop him talking. He looked at the animated compères with an expression of complete astonishment.

'Come on downstairs.'

Trev's den was as Ricky remembered, except it seemed to hold even more tech trash. Like his folks upstairs, Trev threw nothing out. Obsolete televisions, video machines, radios, stereos, all variously dismantled, marooned consumer wreckage of the past decades. Who would ever want this stuff? No one.

'Take a pew. As I said, I did what I could.'

'Thanks, mate.' Ricky handed him the envelope.

Trevor handed back the phone. 'It was pretty fucked, Ricky. All that time out in the elements. No numbers or anything. All I could get out of it was her answering message. It's something, I guess. At least you've got her voice.' Trevor pulled out of a drawer a miniature cassette recorder. 'You can keep this.'

He pressed a button: 'Hi, this is Em. TTYL.' She had a cutesy voice, but oddly sexy too, like a child Marilyn Monroe.

'TTYL. What does that mean?'

'Talk to you later. It's text jargon from the old pop-up phones, before keyboards. Like LOL.'

'Okay. I'll see if this helps us at all.'

'Who's "us"?'

'Myself and a copper who's handling the case, Cade.'

'Name rings a bell.' He sipped his tea. 'Right. There was a piece in

The Mercury couple of months back about a policeman receiving a bravery award for nabbing some bikie drug ord. Arrested him under fire in the clubhouse. It was this guy, Cade.'

'How do you remember something like that?'

'Dad was a copper when I was a kid. I always wanted to be one too. I read all the police stories. Listen in from time to time, I can tune in to their radio signals. All the shit. Drugs and domestics. Helps while away the small hours. How well do you know this guy?'

'Not at all.'

'Perhaps you should walk away from all this Ricky. Drugs. Bikies. You don't want to end up in a wheelchair yourself.'

'I don't know. Probably telling Cade is enough. I feel guilty about this client, Gertrude. Like I could have done something, although I don't know what. One of God's innocents, Trev. A beautiful person like they don't make any more. It's too horrible if someone's killed her.'

'If they really have killed her, mate, it's serious shit. Your business, but at this point I'd be leaving it well alone.'

Ricky is cruising too quickly out along the Lyell Highway, passing all the plodders, the river flashing/glittering manically on his right, the speed jigging/jerking in his head, out to New Norfolk where he has agreed to meet Inspector Cade. Despite his anxiety, it feels good to be moving. The highway hums beneath his new tyres, hums up right through his system. A week since his sacking and he's been on the pills continuously, no sleep at all, trying to deal with it, trying to deal with all manner of things.

Two texts. First Trev, warning him off Cade, talk he heard on the long wave, nothing concrete, just some other cop mouthing off; they probably slagged one another all the time like any workplace. And then Cade himself: 'Meet U Willow Court, Mon. 2 p.m. Nurses Quarters. Sumthing 4 U. TTYL.' TTYL: Emily's acronym. Funny thing for a grown cop to message. Or is it? Maybe this stuff is still used by people who do a lot of messaging. Emily was scared of Willow Court. Why? Something for you. What?

Has to be connected with criminality and drugs. Does Cade want to show him some addicts in their degenerate habitats to make some kind of point? To scare him off? Or, more threateningly, introduce some scarred and tattooed muscled drug lord or hollow-cheeked brown-toothed dealer for the same reason. Whatever it is, Ricky feels compelled to find out, and perhaps draw a line under Gertrude's death and her relationship with the little girl.

He idles in second up New Norfolk's main drag, typical country town Tassie, a little more affluent with the proximity to Hobart and the tourist trade. Still, the dusty second-hand emporiums, clothes and antiques, the newsagency, Masonic Hall, post office, the gun shop… Following his phone – the strange disembodied voice of Siri leading him on – he turns left, and drives between a McDonald's and a Woolworths, across a rattling metal bridge, through two ruined sandstone pillars and suddenly he is in a completely different world, the little stream sharply dividing the modern from the colonial. It seems bizarre. He brakes and looks back through the pillars at the smart bright Maccas and Woolies, both emblematic of cut-price consumerist modernity. But in front of him and around him lies a dream, or nightmare.

He drives on. The road is crumbling, breaking up. Big old deciduous trees lining the road are all winter-stripped, stark and bare. Beyond them, institutional buildings from various eras are in partial or complete ruin. The nurses' quarters: here it is. Ricky is a little late, but no Wade, no other car. He pulls in next to the faded antique sign, switches off the ignition and sits there. He listens to the ticking of the engine and is reminded of visiting Gertrude back in early autumn, at the beginning of this business. What business? He doesn't know. A jumble of facts dances in his brain. Once again, he tries to assemble them, see a pattern.

'Are you trying to make yourself believe this or something?' Yes, no doubt Jackie was right all along: Gertrude died by accident. But by stubbornly believing otherwise, by believing in the evil, Ricky has conjured it up anyway, placing himself here in some real crime scenario. But then who are the criminals? And where is Cade?

He can't sit any longer. He gets out of his car and a freezing wind whacks into him. He reels with the drug and fatigue, almost falling over. A bitter day for a bitter place. The nurses' quarters is a rambling two-storeyed brick Edwardian structure fronted by a flagstone terrace. A few scraggly hens strut and pick at weeds growing through the cracks. He kicks some dry leaves and they scatter squawking. There is no glass in the arched windows and big ragged holes in the masonry. Ricky walks up the entrance steps and on into an airy hall. The timber floor is partly covered in worn lino and partly collapsed. Graffiti defaces the walls, all of it as per usual focused on the genital-urinary: offers, taunts, boasts, insults…shit, cock, fuck, suck, cunt, those punchy little words, literature of the underground, desire and self-loathing, changeless through the ages. He wanders from room to room and scans them, vainly hoping for some hint or clue as to why he is here. There are occasional signs of arson, or maybe people just trying to keep themselves warm. Smell of wet burnt wood and rot. Vermin droppings litter the floor, spiders nest in the corners.

He stands before a closed door. Is it locked? What is behind it? An addict, or a corpse of an addict? The skin on his scalp prickles. Something, he knows. He turns the handle, opens it slowly towards him, and suddenly a pigeon flaps out scaring him out of his wits. It bumps frantically back through the rooms, finally finding an exit. Ricky enters, panting from shock, nerves wound tight to snapping. A mattress spotted with black mould, some defunct gear, needles, piping, stuff he doesn't recognise. A druggie has lived here. There is a strange sweet smell in the air, maybe from the weeds and grass breaking through the floor. Plastic bags are taped over the broken windows, flapping in the breeze. This is how the bird got in and got trapped. There is a smaller room annexed. Also empty except for an ancient wooden hobby-horse. So, a child's room, once.

Willow Court is a place of death and suffering, that is evident. People over a long period have come here and suffered and died and passed this on to the place which now holds that as its identity, so now it attracts those associated with death and suffering, and the whole business perpetuates. That it is all gradually falling to pieces doesn't affect this momentum. The identity of the place, its particular pall, seems to him at this moment stronger than ever, and Ricky feels how great and sustained suffering might lodge itself into a material structure which contains it. No one, nothing can ever scrub the stains from these walls. And if the walls could speak, aside from the graffiti, a commonplace, but still, just imagine all the crazy utterings, the outbursts, cries, one after another, echoing down through the decades. In winter, the bleak wind howling; in summer, the endless monotony of the crickets.

He retreats from the rooms and steps sideways into a breezy corridor leading him back towards the entrance. The wind seems to be driving him down this tunnel which ends, strangely, in a solid iron door, half ajar, which Ricky edges around into a space the width of the corridor, cut from it.

An old metal bed frame, nothing more. One high barred window, the glass smashed. It must have been an isolation cell. The sense of suffering feels particularly powerful here. He stands still for a while, taking it in. All external noise seems to have ceased. Silence, but not absence. On the contrary, there is a weight in the stagnant air. And cold. He starts shivering and slaps his arms and stretches up to look through the window which, across the weed-choked terrace, faces the road. A cold crimson sunset burns his eyes. Gradually it illumines the cell bloody red – he drifts with the spectacle, the sensation – then it fades. He focuses in and then suddenly notices his car is no longer there.

Ricky blinks in amazement. Definitely he parked next to the sign. Someone has just stolen or moved his car, and as that weird fact strikes him, he intuits a movement behind and turns to see the door easing shut with a little sigh. He races over but cannot budge it. Could the wind shift something so solid, so heavy? He cannot tell if it is locked or jammed, but he is trapped. He pulls out his mobile. There is no reception, not even at the window. What to do? He cannot think through the tiredness and the drug. Now he is anxious, his head is buzzing wildly. He sits down on the edge of the bed to try and clear his mind, work out the situation. It feels good just to sit. He wraps his thin jacket tighter around him. He should have stayed in the car. He hangs his head between his knees and something catches his eye from under the bed. He reaches below and picks up a single silver glittering M. The sticky back is covered in filth. He stares stupefied at the shiny letter lying in the crease of his palm.

Yes, surely, this is what Cade wanted him to see. And slowly through the fatigue, through the drug, it takes form: Emily Nettlefold came as an emissary from Gertrude's sister to tell Gertrude that her sister needed her and could not wait any longer. That is it. He rubs his thumb over the glitter. But what he cannot understand is what the girl now wants with him.

The Wild Horses

Rome, capital of emperors and popes, hub of European history and culture. So long Madeleine had dreamed of being here, ever since far-off schoolgirl Latin days. The Forum, the Vatican, Michelangelo, Raphael, Bernini…each successive crisp autumn day minted anew for her while Robert attended his conference. And yet, and yet she remained flat and unmotivated, unable to be astonished by all these astonishing things.

Armed with her apps, she dutifully roamed palaces, observed sculptures and paintings, and…well, nothing much. Maybe her expectations had been so sky-high that some kind of advance unconscious reaction had set in, although it had never happened to her before. Giddy excitable Madeleine Bach, it was so unlike her not to be thrilled, not to be tripping over herself with enthusiasm. Just as well Robert never asked her about her day when he returned, for it would be such a wearying effort for her to dredge it all up again, try and fake what she did not feel.

Something was wrong with her, but what? What to do? Just plug on until she finally snapped out of whatever, store away the multitude of impressions in the hope she would draw on them profitably times hence.

Post-conference, they hired a car, a flashy Maserati no less. Robert said he had done Rome as a backpacker student, couldn't be bothered with it all again – she was grateful for that – then he drove them both at breakneck speed, just like the locals, down the old Appian Way until Madeleine couldn't handle it any more and made him pull up so she could take the wheel. No talk. Robert fiddled endlessly with his phone, just like he did these days at home. The plan was to tour down the coast to Naples and then Amalfi, but the souped-up vehicle overheated and its engine stopped outside Terracina, where the highway met the Tyrrhenian Sea. Madeleine vaguely remembered Terracina also from high school Latin days.

They rang an emergency number the hire car company had provided, and miraculously within an hour a tow truck appeared. The mechanic was a striking curly-headed youth, almost a boy, his beauty marred by a wall-eye. No English. Madeleine managed with her Google Italian, Robert left her to it, and they accepted a lift into town with the car. A water leak. The mechanic's father's garage could replace the tube by tomorrow, they were assured.

Courtesy of the garage, they found themselves installed in a crumbling *pensione*, eating stale pizza and drinking rough chianti in its dark and dingy dining room surrounded by unwashed plates and cutlery, their unpacked bags beside them. Apparently, they were lucky to find it. There was a big soccer match on in town and everything was booked out. Crowds of youths with flags surged up and down the streets, shouting, singing, fighting.

As she chewed on a crust, Madeleine read to Robert from a pamphlet with bleached photos lent to them by their hosts, dating from the sixties. "'For anyone coming from Rome, everything changes quite suddenly at Terracina. One has the impression of entering a country outside time, except that the huge wall overhanging the sea and the city, topped by the mighty temple of Jove, reminds us of the ancient history of Terracina, city of the Volsci. The Via Appia used to pass over the Acropolis up there, Terracina was the key to this highway. Anyone holding Terracina held the Gate of the Sun.' Let's check it out before we leave tomorrow,' she said.

Her husband shrugged, eyes on his phone.

They couldn't sleep with the noise of the soccer celebrations, so they set off early. It was grey dawn and cold, a stiff wind blowing persistently from the sea. They walked towards the sea then climbed steeply up a wide rocky path to the temple, around which was the ancient slum area of the town. This was traditional, Madeleine reflected; poorer areas always used to be in the older precincts of European cities until the tourist trade pushed them elsewhere. But she and Robert were the only tourists here, ridiculously conspicuous, followed at a set distance by a raggedy group of urchins with gaping mouths.

A splendid courtyard fronted the temple of Jove, much of which remarkably still stood intact. Massive marble flagstones, elegant columns. What builders the Romans had been. The Gate of the Sun.

A boy approached them from the urchins.

'He just wants money, Maddie.'

But it seemed he had a story to tell, his tourist English supplementing her Italian. A wall behind his grandfather's house had collapsed and amongst the rubble was a sculpture. Would they like to see it?

'Come on, Rob. It will be an adventure. We've got hours to kill.'

Robert rolled his eyes. The boy had already moved to a back corner of the square, signalling them expectantly.

'Maddie!'

'I want to see what he wants to show us.'

'Jesus!'

She followed the boy, knowing Robert would have to follow her. They were led briskly along a bewildering sequence of paths cut directly into the rock, always rising, until finally they arrived at a sort of furnished cave, in front of which an ancient sat dozing on a cardboard suitcase. Was this his home? Bald pate, sunken cheeks.

'Nonno!'

The man quickly looked up at them, then at his grandson, and rose to his feet. Without a word, he climbed nimbly to a level above the cave where there was a makeshift storage shed with a huge rusty padlock. He unlocked it, pulled back the door and beckoned all inside towards a slab propped against the back, a classical frieze of some sort, Madeleine saw. They all stood in silence before it.

The block, about one metre by two, was incomplete, both ends were jagged, and obviously from some much larger work. White marble, like the landscape all around. It had been cleaned carefully, by the boy or the man, gleaming in the shadow of the shed as though lit from within. It simply showed wild horses galloping left to right. Simply, but Madeleine wondered if she had ever seen anything so ravishing and moving. The details, forelocks and fetlocks, exquisitely rendered, the arched backs, strained withers, corded necks, dilated nostrils. Each beast, and the ensemble, a wonder. The work of a great artist. You might have stared at it for hours, you might have stared at it all your life, as perhaps the original patron had done. Which genius created this? What else did he do? Who would know? Freedom, exultation, grace, strength, energy. Freedom above all. She looked and looked, the casual sweep of muscle and sinew…

And she was eighteen months back.

'There!'

A herd of brumbies sporting on the horizon. In the dusk, with their moulded forms highlighted against the fading sky, they presented as a moving frieze, their fluid interactions as if they were underwater. To Madeleine, they were mythical creatures, the brumbies of the high country, celebrated in verse and song, *The Man from Snowy River* and all that. An anachronistic Australia, a maudlin memory, she knew Robert would say. But what he said was…

'They're doomed, you know,' snuggling his head into her neck. The rub of his bristles suddenly aroused her.

Of course she knew. A longstanding ecological debate that surfaced in the media periodically, one still in progress although the eventual end not in doubt. As she watched the shifting shapes from the snug warmth of the Kosciusko Hotel's bay window, their fate lent them a poignancy, added to the myth. They had revelled in their freedom for almost two centuries, but yes, shortly there would be a final round-up, or maybe worse. Still, for this time of her honeymoon, she could enjoy the occasional spectacle of these superb beasts ranging across the high wild landscape that they had made their home. Even then, she had imagined herself sometime hence, in a stuffy Sydney suburb, reading of their demise, and saw herself remembering back to her and Robert, caught in their net of passionate love.

'What will you do with it?' she asked the old man carefully. She was sure her Italian was correct, but it wasn't clear he understood, perhaps he only spoke dialect.

He shrugged, and answered incomprehensibly.

The boy said, 'You like?'

'*Si, molto bello.*' Was that right?

Did the man want to sell it to them? He was an uneducated peasant but of course he could see what anyone could, this block, in itself, was a little masterpiece, a decontextualised fragment from some complete masterpiece, itself part of a mostly unimaginable world.

Madeleine could sense Robert's impatience. She paced back and forth slowly in front of the frieze, trying to take it in. What was she trying to take in? What did we have here? A chilly windswept morning in a nondescript Italian town. A young couple from halfway around the world. A poor man and his grandson. And one random precious detail from a lost civilisation; isolate, anonymous.

Now the old man was nodding his head like an idiot goat, except that his eyes were blazing with greed. The boy stood by non-committal, a little embarrassed, tracing the dirt with a stick.

'Come on, Maddie, let's go. We can't buy it or anything, we're just wasting their time.'

Ever the voice of reason. She wondered how the story would eventually play out, whether somehow these two could ever manage to turn this incredible find to some recompense. Probably not, almost certainly not; they were too powerless. She and Robert should leave, they had to leave, but still, still, Madeleine just could not take her eyes off this thing, glimpse of some magnificent greater whole which had gone and could never be recovered.

The Ultimate Economy

Raising his eyes from the desk's finely tooled leather veneer, Stephen sees that his familiar office furnishings have assumed a kind of unreality. He considers something new: the world as absurd. Which nudges him slightly from his grief, although it is fully there, along with a physical pain in his throat and chest. The heart, that perennially sensitive organ.

He stands, right leg numb, needles and pins, waits for restored sense, then limps out the office door, carefully locking it as ever, and over to the lift lobby. Up to the top floor and the short steep flight of metal steps leading to the roof. The safety rod seems unnaturally cold. He pushes open the outsized security door (Authorised Personnel Only), and steps down onto wet concrete.

It was raining when he first read the email. Now it has cleared. Behind scattered cumulus, a few stars shine, a mild spring night, slightly fragrant after the rain, even here in the coil of the city. Remote traffic noises meld into a general hum of life. Around him is the baroque paraphernalia of the antiquated air conditioning system, also humming. Stephen meant to itemise its upgrading at the last board meeting. Another little matter he has failed to address.

He weaves through this to the edge. He was right. It is simple. A flimsy railing. The street is empty and appears a long way down. Fifty storeys. When he first started working here, many years back, this was one of the tallest buildings in the city, a prestigious address. Looking down, he is both exhilarated and fearful and a sensation lodges in his genitals that he has always felt at heights. Probably something to do with balance. Also the common fantasy of launching off. Now he will do this. He must ensure that he jumps well clear of the building. He buttons up his suit coat.

''Scuse me, mister!'

Always someone! Stephen turns and there perched on an air conditioning tube is a woman, maybe in her mid-thirties, obviously a derelict of some kind, crazy or substance-abuser or both. She is an apparition as odd as unexpected, swathed in a filthy array of brightly hued overlapping cloths, some personal couture of odds and ends, like an oversize tropical bird. Although she is in shadow, all her physical details seem sharp as though he is seeing her through a suddenly focused lens.

'Lovely evening,' he responds ludicrously, his voice sounding to him as if spoken by someone else. He can jump when she moves on, or just walk around to the other side of the building. No need to distress her.

'What you say?'

'Lovely evening.'

'What?'

'The evening.'

'You got the time?'

He slips out his phone. No messages.

'Ten thirty.'

'Why you workin' so late?'

Why was he working so late?

'Do I know you, mister?'

'No!' But he does seem to recognise her voice. Maybe he's regularly walked past her without noticing. On the footpath with a sign or something. So many people in a life, even a truncated one. He peers closer. 'What are you doing up here, madam?'

'I'm going to kill meself.'

'Well, don't let me stop you!' What is he saying? He is not in control. But wait, did he hear right?

'Tell me again,' he says.

'Just makin' a few last calculations. Numbers never lie.' (Is that true?) 'Ten thirty, you say.'

Stephen moves in to examine this strange doppelganger. She is intently bent over a book, jabbing at it sharply with a pen or pencil. Older than he first thought, but how old is difficult to say. For while her body looks relatively young, the skin on her face is like very worn, soft leather. A lifetime of outdoors. Her ash-blonde hair is loosely gathered up in a crimson scarf. He can smell her now, sweat and urine.

He clears his throat. 'Well, I'm going to kill myself too.'

At that, she stops her jabbing and stares at him in unblinking silence, mouth open, jaws working back and forth. There is a glaze of saliva on her chin. Time passes.

'I've just learned my wife and closest friend are lovers.'

Was she waiting for an explanation? Why has he offered one?

'I sorta thought that type of thing went on all the time.'

'Not to me.'

Meeting her stare, he recalls how from incomprehension, through incredulity, bewilderment, shock, jealousy and anger, he had arrived at the final station: grief. The end of the line. A slow succession of tears had flowed silently down his cheeks like a miraculous statue, blotching the leather veneer. He had not cried since boyhood, when he had cried regularly and copiously. On the day-by-day desk calendar, beneath his note to buy cat food, was a dictum of Aristotle's: 'The unexamined life is not worth living'. Until the email, Stephen would have thought this ridiculous, unmanly even. But with Aristotle's cue he had found himself forcing himself, a compulsion both voluntary and involuntary, through a complete reappraisal of his entire adult life, the only part of his life that had seemed of any worth.

Their faces had materialised in the office gloom, almost hallucinatory. Joyce's, thin and fine, with large close-set chestnut eyes, like a deer's, he'd always fancied, gentle but not tame, and with a wild animal's secretiveness. Whereas Craig's was the opposite, open and frank, a little flushed from his drinking, hail-fellow-well-met, a natural charmer's façade, behind which naturally also lay secrets. Then Stephen's brain had kicked into an unstoppable sequence of memories of Joyce, Joyce and himself, Joyce and Craig and himself.

Could he identify any specific incident where betrayal was obvious?

No. So then every act, even the innocent, must now appear guilty. The whole picture irreparably foxed.

'You goin' to punish them.'

'… Maybe.'

'Ya reckon they're worth it?'

'Probably not.'

'Probably they don't give a rat's.'

'It doesn't matter. There's nothing left.'

She snorts at this, which riles him somewhat.

'So why are you killing yourself?''

She brandishes the book at him. 'Save money.'

'What?'

'It's costin' me too much to live.'

Maybe she isn't crazy. She seems serious, not at all hysterical. People do kill themselves for rational reasons.

Stephen feels a burst of sympathy. 'Listen, I'm well off, I've nothing further to live for, believe me. I really am going to kill myself. I have my wallet here. There's some cash, cards. At least you won't be poor for a while.'

Craig always his closest friend, especially throughout their wretched boyhood with the Brothers. Were those men still alive? Impossible. Warriors of Christ. Christ almighty! Here were the bloody demons all right; you had to conjure the angels yourself. Survival meant holding in, first lesson, at which he was not good. But when Craig arrived, they bonded instinctively, perhaps only as children can, a bond that grew as they grew and suffered. The Monday morning they met, chatting casually in the library under Father Dominic's baleful watch. A morning of bright winter sun. Craig, a man so easy in his own skin, unlike himself. So much he had learnt from him, admired in him. Their success together a realisation wildly beyond boyhood dreams, although of course, largely through his own initiative and effort.

But then so typical of Craig's carelessness (casualness?) to send a personal file with a batch of business rubbish. The writing itself, intense and passionate, he found difficult to imagine from Joyce, although unmistakably it was hers. Certainly he had never received anything in any form from her vaguely resembling this, in fact had never sought it, and almost incidentally was surprised to discover her capable of such range and depth of emotion. The cursor blinking at him impersonally. Do you want to shut down? Yes.

'Ain't poor now.'

'What?'

'Your hearin' crook, mate?'

'You said you were killing yourself because it costs too much to live.'

'Right.'

'Well?'

'What?'

'I'm offering you money.'

'Don't want it. Make my problem worse.'

'What's your problem?'

'Savin'.'

'Saving for what?'

'You see mister, I 'ate spendin', 'ate to think that what's mine has got to go to some other bastard.'

The cars, the clothes, the holidays, anything she wanted, even before they were married. He needed her to ask him. Yes, clearly he'd been papering over a gap. Her sequence of notes suggested some of this largesse had been diverted to Craig. A not uncommon business bind, as it happens, money thrown at a problem, funding, not solving, that problem.

'But then if, as you claim, you've plenty of money, what does it matter?'

'It matters. 'Ad nothin' when I was a kid. I was a orphan. Just you try and think of that, you being rich and all. I learned what it was to be 'ungry, learned how to scrimp and save. 'Ad to bludge food. Steal it sometimes. No easy ride for me, mister. But you know, as time went on, I found I 'ad a real natural talent for savin' and bludgin', a gift, if I don't say so meself. I got along. No easy ride, but I got along. Bit of a natural.' She breaks into a violent cackle, then hawks loudly. 'Bernadette's me name.'

'Stephen.'

Are they worth it? Are they worth his life, that's what she was asking. But the question he was asking was, does he still love them? The answer was, is, yes, of course. Life seems inconceivable without them as he is and always has been bound to them. So an evasion, is that what he is about? No doubt. An evasion of life. And what have been life's highest finest moments? Making love to Joyce, no, the deep calm after making love to her, even if, he must admit it now, and its implications, he more than occasionally sensed his feeling not reciprocated.

All he thought was his is now theirs, is no longer, perhaps never was. He has attempted to construct a complete life out of nothing, and it seems that the effort, enormous for him, enormous for anyone really, has not been finally successful. The walls of his beloved home have atomised from the heat of some immense alien passion. It is monstrous, inexplicable, yet it must be accounted for. He must account for it, for in some tangential way he is partly responsible for it.

'…and I was a bit of a looker in my time too, so I made sure I hooked a good earner. Not that I ever let 'im spend any of it. Watched 'im with skinned eyes. Never wasted a penny. Only bought things on special. Search through the papers for hours for bargains, wait in line for hours to pick 'em up. Vinnies clothes, shoes from the tip, I 'ad it all down pat, economies of scale, economies of use, every way I could possibly avoid spendin'. Jim was always sayin', "Let your hair down a bit" but no fuckin' way. I says to 'im, "You never been poor. You don't know what's what." But 'e used to spend money anyway, fucked if I know 'ow, you know, without me knowin', though I'd always find 'im out in the end, after I'd done me sums. Ain't the bastard born can pull one over me.'

She pauses for another extravagant hawk, followed by a protracted bout of spitting and coughing. So she is crazy, but is she serious? Maybe this is some kind of regular act, and he needs to work out from her what part he must play. To break the spell.

'Anyway, I quickly comes to realise you can't really save, not proper like, with another body around eatin' from the same plate as you. But there I was. Nothin' I could do about it, 'cause he made the money you see, just keep watchin' 'im. Then one day, 'e dies, just like that, stroke, and I thinks, well, I don't want his money, I can save better on me own, in peace, with no worries about some other bastard wastin' it. Whatever it is, it's mine, no one else can spend it. Well, I 'ad quite a pile when Jimmy croaked. Always fightin' with the bank over the interest, and the fuckin' tax man! I 'ad me pension and me interest, but they were me rightful due, I'd be buggered if I was goin' to spend them. So I started hoardin' stuff, you know, shopliftin' and like. I never bought any new clothes at all, new anythin'. I sold me 'ouse and moved into a little room. I never went out. If you go out, it costs money. Began eatin' pet food.'

'What's it like?'

'What?'

'Pet food. I've always wondered.'

''Orrible, but it saves. Anyway, I did everything I could, every fuckin' thing, but I was still spendin'. It was gettin' away from me. I don't know 'ow. I'd dream about it, you know. I just couldn't see where it was goin'. Drove me crazy! Then one night I 'ad a vision. God 'elp me! All at once it come to me what 'ad been costin' me money all these bloody years. I 'ad the answer right 'ere in the palm of me 'and. Know what it was?'

'Tell me.'

'Livin', mister. Livin' costs. You can scrimp and save for all your fuckin' worth but while you're livin' you're spendin'. There ain' nothin' you can do about it, except stop livin'!'

'But if you kill yourself now, what good will all your saving be to you, all that effort?'

'I don't care about that! I just can't stand to spend any more!'

'You're telling me you're going to kill yourself simply to save money? That's ridiculous!'

'Mister, you look after your death, and I'll look after mine.'

'Let me get this totally straight: you're going to kill yourself purely as an economy measure, right?'

'Right.'

'Well, what about this: if you kill yourself now, you'll never again know the joy of saving.'

'There ain't no more savin' I can do, mate, except this.'

'But it's such a waste!'

'It's the wastin' I'm tryin' to stop! I can see I'm getting' nowhere with you. 'Ere, 'old this.' She rises from her perch, approaches Stephen along with her stench, and hands him a soiled spiral-bound exercise book.

He flicks through it. The pages are covered in flamboyant numerical ciphers, all contained within neat red-ink double-margin lines. He examines them; none of them seem to add up.

'I was just sittin' here quietly, workin' out 'ow much I was goin' to save a week by doin' this. But it don't come to very much.' She shakes her head. ''Ardly worth it.' She snatches back the book and strides to the edge.

'No!'

But she's gone! And he is shocked to his core! Horrified! How stupid! He leans over the railing but cannot locate her. Still, she couldn't have possibly survived. He takes it in.

All right, she was crazy, but surely he could have talked her out of it. Surely he could have done something! The money, he shouldn't have offered it. He can't imagine how anything else would have made any difference, but it wasn't the answer. He hadn't learnt his part in time, whatever it was.

Suddenly he feels exhausted. He turns and slumps back against the railing. The pain in his chest and throat has eased. He listens to the night, the hum, then slips out his phone, rings triple-O and reports the suicide. The voice is shaky but it is his. It is a lovely evening. He pulls the printed email from his coat pocket, reads it again, steels himself – the phone is still in his hand – sucks in a deep draught of spring air, and calls his solicitor.

The Idol

Dianne had often envisaged leaving Griff, when he thoughtlessly upset her or for some reason things weren't going right between them, although never seriously. I was just a kind of escape valve, one of many in dealing with a long-term relationship. But when he, right out of the blue, got up and left her, she was totally blindsided. Gobsmacked.

An 'unplanned leave' day manically scouring the house top to bottom – skirting boards, windowsills, kitchen pantry, never had it been this clean – she then wandered back out into her well-ordered well-bordered world in an uncomprehending daze, knocking against the furniture, tripping on the footpath, forgetting routine work duties. It was a kind of grief, she realised, not grief like an actual death, but still, here was a metaphoric death, a genuine loss, and through that daze Dianne gradually began to see more clearly how she was mourning not so much for Griff and what they had had together, but more for what they might have had that never eventuated.

For, in truth, particularly recently, the relationship had become stale, threadbare. She couldn't even remember the last time they'd had sex. They hardly spoke to one another, even went separately to the cinema, once their big mutual passion. They had lost the knack of intimacy. But still, never she could have foreseen her and Griff, Griff and her, being apart, simply because they had been so long together.

In fact, for over half her life. Dianne was now forty-two. She had met Griff aged eighteen at a student party; they were both Film Majors, serious cinephiles, and they had chatted on till dawn. But they were good friends before they were lovers, in a group household, and maybe in some way that lay at the root of it, for there had never been the unuttered hope and blazing spark, just cohabitation with sex then thrown in. So they had never taken the thing as seriously as they might, invested what they should; always there was this idea, lurking unseen, that each was free to go their own way if and when they chose, although neither of them had, until now. And just as nothing in particular had engendered the relationship, there also seemed to be no outstanding reason, or any reason at all, for Griff's departure.

He had left a note, maddeningly brief. He had ever been a man of few words, like many men, unlike herself, and actually this was a gender novelty Dianne had always found attractive, natural taciturnity, which she, probably falsely, interpreted as self-possession. Then again, it was a trait that obviously might (and did) cause problems in a relationship. On to the final problem, his absence, Griff characteristically enigmatic: 'Time to move on for me. Sorry, Di. I've taken a job in Adelaide.' Adelaide? He'd never been there in his life. Well, far as she knew.

All her calls went to message bank, her texts, emails, all unanswered, and then she stopped. Oddly, they had never discussed marriage or children, things that might have bonded them more. Why? She never had the guts is why, suspecting, worrying, that either prospect would push him away. Now he was away anyway, and it was too late for her to have a family. She could probably find another partner, she was still slim and attractive, she knew, but one big possibility of life for her had inadvertently slipped by. When she dwelt on it, anger boiled up, at him, but also at herself. She had spent, wasted, over half her life with a man she had maybe never really loved – she wasn't entirely sure on that point – in a manifestly unequal relationship she had nevertheless taken completely for granted. Now she had nothing.

Not even property. They had always rented, it was another unspoken feature of the 'deal', the no-real-ties, she'll-be-right, we can live in a better place, dine at smart restaurants, buy nice clothes, travel, and anyway we have one another, it's enough. Obviously not. Dianne felt totally hollowed out, angry, betrayed, all those things, but of course, she had let herself into this, gone along for the ride. She had made her bed and now had to lie in it, by herself.

And that was another weird thing: now that she could no longer have sex with Griff, she wanted it, needed it. Probably for comfort or self-esteem. She began recalling their various sexual encounters and habits down the years; idling at work or waiting at the bus stop, defunct erotic images would pop into her mind. Then she started imagining Griff having sex with other women. She couldn't see the other women, or woman, only Griff, his moves which she knew so intimately, what they had enacted together, which surely had to be more powerful and meaningful than with this other woman. Why? No reason. Nonsense. Well, at least she'd shifted from herself to someone else, a progression of sorts. Or was it? Most likely he was with no one. It was all crazy.

In the streets, she caught herself looking at couples. They seemed to be everywhere. Where had they all come from? Better to stay home. But as she shuffled around the empty house, doing this, doing that, dishes, washing, dusting, she'd forget Griff wasn't there, set two plates, make space in the wardrobe, avoid playing music he didn't like. Then she'd catch herself and would have to sit down and claw back. He was present, he was absent. Like a phantom limb; part of her had been lopped off but her brain hadn't fully processed this and was still regis-tering response. Or she was an actor who had not learnt her updated role and had been caught 'going through the motions', that shopworn phrase. How apt it was.

One positive, sort of: he had walked out leaving pretty much all their possessions, taken his clothes and that was it. He'd organised his move the weekend she was in Launceston for her mother's birthday, planned it all in advance. Well, he had to if he was going to skedaddle without so much as a word, and a job and all. The books, CDs, DVDs, the lounge suite, the bloody bed, presumably it was now all hers. But of course it all reminded her of him. He'd got rid of her but she couldn't get rid of him.

'He left you his stuff as well?' This was Marianne, her oldest friend, going back to kinder, who Dianne had always suspected of having a thing for Griff, and was no doubt enjoying some schadenfreude amongst her genuine sympathy. She was fine, rock-solid husband, good earner, bit dull, played golf every Saturday, but still, around, mostly, plus three bonny boys, five, three, two. Who this Saturday morning (Richard on the green), were proving quite a handful in their different ways. Would she really have been up for this? But boys are always a problem. Or, the problem.

'Yeah, I mean it's all mixed up with mine. We shared everything. There's a heap of junk in the basement.'

'Basement? Can you still afford the rent here?'

'Couple of months, then I'm going to have to move.'

'Okay, Di, you need to go through this stuff and work out what you want and start throwing the rest out. You need to purge. First step in making a new start: getting your shit together. Then you move. Then you find another man.'

'I don't know if I want another man. Certainly not for a while. The other, though, yes, you're right. I do need to tackle it. I'll start this weekend.'

'That's my Di.'

Yes, she definitely missed his physical presence. One big reason Dianne had hooked up with Griff originally was that he was so damn attractive. All her girlfriends had mooned after him, so that when he started paying her attention, she felt he was too good an opportunity to pass up. Then she became addicted.

She remembered how she had marvelled at his long sleek form, his beautiful hands and back and thighs that belonged just to her. After a while, she felt at the mercy of his face and body. Which was the first step in engendering a sense of inequality between them, so that gradually, casually, also very naturally, it seemed – although she could and did note it as it was occurring – he began to dominate her. Not sexually, but personally. Dianne felt powerless to prevent it. She was not experienced enough, or strong enough. Griff was the original adored spoilt child, charismatic and confident, always with the knack of knowing the right thing to do or say. His whole life all the people he had known –

parents, teachers, friends – had deferred to him, and therefore so must she. His looks, and the rest, were an armour she could not crack.

Dianne had chafed at the unfairness, but came to see that these were the only terms on which the relationship could survive, because it was how all Griff's relationships had evolved – never had he known anything different. If she wanted him, she must accept them. So it went on. In everything, his beauty and self-possession gave him the advantage. Her present jealous fantasies were probably founded on the truth that Griff would have no problem whatever picking up a much younger partner and having the family he was not going to have with her.

'What you need is three piles: things you want, things you don't, and undecided.'

Why was she listening to this?

'Tell me, Marianne, do you think there might have been another woman?

'Nothing I ever heard of. He was a dish. Still is, I guess. You know, honestly, I don't think he was the type.'

As soon as she heard her friend say this, Dianne knew it was right. The women were no doubt there, as opportunity presented, but infidelity would have been too complicated, too fraught for Griff, too much effort all round for the reward. He liked a simple life, no pressures, no worries. If he wanted sex, he could always screw her, not that, generally speaking, he was particularly motivated. A 'once-a-week' man at most. More often than not, Dianne had to initiate proceedings. But still, there must have been something she wasn't seeing.

Two coffees, boys' noise, and Marianne's chatter were doing her in. She needed to disengage. She pleaded a headache and took off on a long looping walk through Wentworth Park, which Marianne's faux mansion fronted. Good earner hubby.

Dianne had not been in this park since she couldn't remember. Wild fires were presently burning beyond Mount Wellington down in the Huon valley – there had been weeks of hot dry days – and the air was infused with smoke. The summer light caught all the particles, making it like an unnaturally bright dusk when it was midday. The surface of the river was a sun-illumined turquoise backed by a scree of smoke. Everything was unreal. Everywhere was a strange vacancy. Life had lost a tension. She felt insubstantial. She was responsible only for herself. There were no demands. She could do anything, it didn't matter, nothing seemed to matter. Griff's going had left this great slack gap. Did she need to fill it? She didn't feel the need.

The basement, Saturday night. She'd bought takeaway, butter chicken, gobbled it down, all that salt and grease, and was sitting alone in silence in the empty living room enjoying one of Griff's fine cold Rieslings. This had come from the basement. Of course she would keep all the wine, although it would take her a lifetime to get through it. Boxes of wine, boxes of God-knows-what. How had they accumulated all that stuff? Dianne felt exhausted just thinking about it but, yes, she would make a start tomorrow. What else was she going to do?

Alone in the silence and the space, she sipped her wine.

Truth was, right now she wasn't feeling that bad. Solitude rather than loneliness. In the madly interconnected world everyone lived these days, solitude had been given short shrift. If you weren't constantly occupied, you were missing out, a loser. That was horseshit. Solitude used to be prized. You would need to cultivate it a bit, but still, even at this early stage, Dianne could see how it might become deeply satisfying. And silence, she listened to it, the silence of the large empty room. It was a natural companion to solitude.

It was a pity to have to ditch the house. Dianne had a good job – Film Conservator at the State Library, a job she loved and which would probably see her out – but she couldn't afford this, a stately sandstone Georgian in South Hobart, run-down, mates rates, the owner an uncle of Griff's. But she could enjoy it for a while, the elegant high ceilings, regal proportions. They knew how to make 'em back then. On the other hand, it did represent the 'old' life. If she stayed here, the ghost of Griff, of their shared time, would no doubt haunt and oppress her. And it was too big for one, even leaving aside the cost, really too big for two; she needed something that would fit her better, fit her new life, whatever that would be. She would see out the lease, then go.

So here she was, forty-two. She'd lived half her life, and half of that she was at present not so proud of. It was not the life she could and should have lived. Certain things, important things, had been foregone. But still, there was plenty of time ahead.

No partner, no kids, but even in the short term it opened out other prospects. She could binge on all those quality Netflix and Amazon series she'd never got around to, the whole television-as-the-new-cinematic-art-form thing. And as for film, there was vintage this, classic that, even old TV series, everything. Catch up on what had passed her by over the years, or re-watch what she loved. Go down the alphabet listings section by section: drama, comedy, adventure, thriller, foreign, horror, get totally film literate as she'd always wanted.

Or if she ever tired of film, which she couldn't imagine, she could read, say, Gibbon or Proust. She had always wanted to read Proust. Learn Beethoven's late quartets. Or learn an instrument herself. What about the cello? She loved the cello. If that proved too difficult, she could sing. Join a choir. She had to work, but other than that she could do anything she liked. Which after years of Griff was a strange thought (although she could have done any of those while still with Griff). Or, of course, as Marianne said, because Marianne could imagine nothing else, she might meet another man. Or alternatively, she might do nothing at all. Sit in solitude, like the ancients.

But first she had to clean out the basement.

The basement was actually a cellar. The house, convict-built, dating back to the 1820s, a heritage-listed money pit (not that the uncle was splashing out), was originally owned by a wine and rum merchant, one of the early mountebanks of the colony. She and Griff had lived here for well over a decade and the cellar inevitably had become a junk dump. What did they call it? Decluttering. There was a whole industry, how-to books and everything. A right and wrong approach/method. Throwing out junk as a science.

Dianne had considered hiring a skip but there was simply too much for her to do it in one fell swoop. Little by little would be best. Chip away. It was Sunday morning; she was fresh, primed for action. As she grasped the iron knob handle on the solid slanting door to the stairs, she had a strange feeling of presentiment. Her skin prickled; someone stepping on her grave, as her Gran used to say. Nerves on edge while descending the unsafe wooden slats into the low room, poorly illumined by a single bulb. Why? No reason. Cobwebs in her brain as well as the room. Work would soon dispel all that.

The wine boxes were clearly labelled and grouped together, so that was easy. They could be left for the while. But there were myriad other boxes and suitcases of all shapes and sizes scattered around in the gloom. She had a clutch of bin bags, yellow for keeps, black for not. Aside from the clothes, she needed to choose those things that were her, not Griff, which could tell her who she was without him. Redefine herself through what was previously shared.

Where to start? The suitcases would probably contain clothes, which would be easiest to sort and carry. She took a deep musty breath and set to it with a vengeance, summoning up the manic energy with which she'd attacked the house the day after he'd left. Four hours later, she was clogging the living room with her two piles, by far the larger that for St Vinnies. She knew she also couldn't keep most of the clothes in the yellow bags. Maybe she could give them to relatives or friends or sell them at a market somewhere.

Dianne finished the suitcases, hauled them up too, and paused for a proper break, a sandwich and a cuppa. While she recouped, sanity struck. She didn't want to spend her entire Sunday doing this. There was no need. Another hour on the boxes and she would leave it till next weekend. More than enough up here already to further sort, and somehow disperse.

She plunged back in. Books, CDs, videos, photo albums, old crockery; this was all more labour intensive. She was nearing the end of her energies when she came across an odd wooden box with a lid, that seemed to have nothing in it but screwed-up tissue paper; but nestled deep within the paper was a solid oblong object the size of a forearm, that when unwrapped revealed itself as a stone carving. Dianne held it up in the murky light. It was a figure of a man, legs and torso foreshortened, with a long fierce scowling face. The weight of it seemed unnatural, as though it were denser than the stone from which it was carved.

She recognised it. From where? She looked and looked and slowly realization dawned. It seemed incredible, but the more she looked, the more certain she became.

Dianne had last seen this figure as part of a travelling exhibition, from the New York Metropolitan Museum no less, of pre-Colombian indigenous art. She remembered joking to Griff that this little man's face in some indefinable way resembled his own. When the exhibition had moved on from Hobart, the item was missing. Although naturally the collection was insured, this incident was a major embarrassment at the time for her workplace, the State Library, which had hosted the collection en route to Melbourne, and security was considerably upgraded as a result. That was what, six, seven years ago. And here it was, in her basement, in her hand, the missing artefact.

Griff had nicked it. Incredible! How? Why? She sat on her haunches for a while, dumbfounded, then carried the carving up into the clear light of the house. It looked undamaged. Actually it looked in excellent condition for something so old, the features sharp and expressive. Dianne brought it into her study and placed it next to the computer. Ten minutes later, she knew what it was: a funerary jade figurine from the Mezcala Culture in south-western Mexico, circa 300–100 BC. And more incredibly, what it was worth: three hundred thousand American dollars on the open market. She stared at the figure in amazement and saw a distorted avatar of Griff staring cold-eyed back at her. In mockery? Amusement? Wordless as ever.

'You're looking great. Taken off weight.'

'Actually, I think I've put on a couple of kilos.'

'Put on. Right. Anyway you're obviously thriving without him. Tell you the honest truth, never wanted you to know, obviously, but I didn't really like Griff much, too up himself and all that.'

This was codswallop. Marianne had been totally charmed like everyone.

'Marianne, there's something I wanted to sound you out on.'

'What are friends for?'

'When I was going through the stuff in the basement, I found something that I'm pretty sure Griff stole.'

'Stole? Are you sure? What is it?'

'I can't tell you. It's nothing really important. But I'm not too sure what to do about it.'

'Well, I guess you should return it.'

'I can't.'

'Why?'

'Because it's stolen.'

'I would have thought that would be the reason to return it.'

'I'm worried if I return it, Griff might be charged. Or if he denies any knowledge, I might be. And if that happens, I might lose my job. And there's something else bothering me.'

'Yes?' Marianne was clearly captivated here.

'Why didn't Griff take it with him? What it is, he could hardly have forgotten it.'

'Maybe he felt embarrassed, guilty at what he had done, and couldn't handle keeping it.'

'If that was the case, he could have thrown it away or left it anonymously somewhere. No, I think he wanted me to find it.'

'Are you sure?'

'There's no other logical explanation.'

'But why? What is it?'

It had been a mistake to bring it up with Marianne, but Dianne had been bursting to discuss the business with someone, even in such ridiculously abstract terms. 'All I can say is, I really don't know what's been going on in his head. But if that was his plan, I guess in due course I'll find out.'

'Well, Di, you know I'm always here to talk these things over.'

Dianne had been keeping the idol locked in a drawer, but after a while she considered it unnecessary. No one knew she had the thing, save Griff. No one visited her these days. Why not bring it out and enjoy it, give the little man some air after having been cooped up for so long?

She was well into the habit of the evening silences, just sitting alone after dinner in front of the fireplace doing absolutely nothing. It was March and the air was turning crisp. She began lighting the fire. She and Griff had always ignored it and used the heat pump – organising wood and cleaning the grate seemed too much effort – now Dianne seemed to have time in abundance, and the soft crackle of the flames was a fine accompaniment to the silence. She could sit there contentedly for hours.

It was dusk, the dishes were stacked, and she set the idol beside her on the coffee table next to her comfy fire chair. The flames had settled down, just one large log burning sombrely. There was no internal light save from that, and as the external light gradually waned, as the shadows in the room around her shifted and deepened, the idol began to softly glow of its own accord. No doubt a feature of the jade. Finally, when it was completely dark outside, inside, the log and the idol held luminous conference.

Dianne held herself still, scarcely breathing. What did the idol represent? What properties had been invested in it by those ancient peoples? She fancied she could sense its totemic power. As the night hours drifted on, she further fancied that she herself was drawing some kind of power from it. Just her, the log and the idol, and the spell of deep silence.

Each morning when she woke, she felt, knew, she had been dreaming about the idol, but she could never recall her dreams. Each night,

night after night, she sat before the fire, autumn deepening to winter, all day-work forgotten, her and the fire and the idol, trying to think it through. Why had Griff wanted her to know about it? Why now, after all this time? What was he expecting from her? Was it some kind of test? Yes, surely, Griff had revealed his secret and shameful act – by this object that spoke of it, which also physically recalled him – and was giving her time, all the time she needed, all these long winter nights, to come to some kind of decision, concerning him, or concerning him and her.

Griff leaving the idol for her to discover was an act, but a passive act, that gave her a certain power over him, of possible betrayal. And if betrayal was not followed through, then the business became a bond, like a sort of bond of thievery. The stolen idol bound them together, particularly since it was so valuable, and with the ongoing leverage of her knowledge of his original theft – a more serious crime than her complicity – yes, gave her a power she had never had in their relationship.

The stone glowed.

She remembered once coming across him staring at himself, half-dressed, in their full-length wardrobe mirror. He was absorbed and did not notice her. One odd thing: despite his beauty, and his casual use of it, Griff was not vain, not one of those men always trying to catch sight of themselves reflected elsewhere. This moment he looked at himself almost querulously, head tilted, as though he did not quite understand what he saw, dissatisfied too, she fancied. Maybe, Narcissus-like, he had wished to disappear into his image, if not for Narcissus's reasons, but knew he could not. While she was with him, because of that image, Dianne had not been able to see this.

She regarded the idol, with its perverted Griff face. The idol spoke of another Griff; that's why he had taken it. He also could not work against his charisma, just like all the others, and he saw it was eventually going to wreck his life. He needed a strategy to counteract it. And maybe this other Griff could somehow provide it for him.

She rose from her chair, took the stone up in both her hands, and stared into its depths.

The idol was a statement of his love, and a test of hers. It could enable their relationship to change, and so endure. This was the source of its power, now flowing from it to her. At some point, Griff had grasped, as she now was doing, the agency of this strange talisman.

So finally, when through successive nightly deliberations Dianne had arrived at this poised but equivocal point, one late winter Saturday morning, after she had just lit the fire, there was a familiar knock on the front door. Heart in mouth, she raced over, hardly believing, but sure enough, there on the porch before her, a little thinner and worn, stood Griff.

There was something new in his handsome face, a subtlety, maybe a depth, that either had not been there before or, more likely, she had never noticed. Then a sudden rage possessed Dianne and with her clenched fist, she struck him full in the mouth, a thing she had never done in her life. He took no evasive action, just stood there. She saw that she had pushed in one of his front teeth. He carefully positioned it back in place as the blood welled past his lips, and staunched the flow with the sleeve of his shirt. Dianne saw he had no luggage, not even a backpack. She looked down at her hand which was sore and skinned, throbbing. Griff also looked at it, then took it gently and wordlessly led her back into the house almost as though he'd never left.

She trailed wonderingly. Griff led Dianne directly to the idol beside her fire chair. He picked it up and, still with her in hand, carried it back down to the basement. He carefully repacked the idol, now also smeared with blood, in its wrappings and its box, straightened, and took her hand once more. He led her back up to the fireplace, placed a chair next to hers, and sat there with her, her bloodied hand in his, dabbing his mouth from time to time and staring into the growing flames.

The Sundowners

A midwinter's evening tightened its vice on the squat complex of Happy Valley Nursing Home, hunkered down in a scrappy patch of bush beyond Hobart's northern suburbs. As outside the cold and dark deepened, inside a presence surreptitiously infused the stagnant overheated air, the aromas of institutional food and bodily wastes, finally reaching the dementia residents. The 'sundowning', the hour when those within respond to that without, unbend their arthritic/scoliotic frames and float ethereally, as in some ghastly ghostly dress rehearsal, through the maze of thickly carpeted corridors and empty recreation halls.

'Jesus, once more unto the breach,' Brian Watson muttered out of earshot of tall gaunt Mavis Connell, carriage erect, wafting through the nurses and carers' station, the 'Hub', directly between himself and Helen McDonald. The smudge of her wasted form through a stained diaphanous nightgown, eyes glazed and unfocused, seemingly heading nowhere, but Brian knew, he knew all right, Mavis was seeking exit, any exit in the fortress, heeding the age-old call of the wild.

'At least she's got her pad on. Almost got away last night, didn't you know?'

This was Helen, sharing this shift with him, Wednesday two p.m. to ten p.m., maybe overnight if the relief didn't show, their new enrolled nurse out on exchange. She had a dense Scottish burr and looked directly at Brian looking back at her while he adjusted his ears to what she had said. Didn't seem to mind the male gaze. Maybe it was a cultural thing, like the French. A looker, and knew it. Not that he wanted any work thing. Nevertheless, while tending the ancient wasted bodies in his charge, washing and massaging all those corporal parodies, as in a kind of double vision, Brian had increasingly found himself imagining administering similar attentions to this tight bright form here before him.

'One day she'll have a brain snap and learn the code, maybe let the lot out,' he replied.

'It was Exit West, the one that opens onto the highway. What's the code?'

'For West? Two-two-three-three-hash.'

'You know them all?'

'That's how long I've been here.'

'How long?'

'Too long. So what happened?'

'That lass Sandra was taking out the rubbish and propped the door open so she wouldn't have to go through re-entry procedure. Sheer bloody laziness. She turns around and Mavis is already past her.'

'I wonder where she thought she was going.'

'Mavis told me at lunch she's in Hell and has to get to Heaven.'

'She'll get to Heaven soon enough.' He refilled his tepid coffee from the thermos. 'Let me tell you, I've worked in more hellish places than this.'

'This is better than in Glasgow.'

'Well, they know fuck-all about Glasgow. Or anything. No one comes here willingly. They've all been placed. The only time they can get out is when we take them to the doctor to get their meds renewed. And we're right with them like jailors. Did you write up an incident report on Sandra?'

'Should I? She's new like me, isn't she?'

'You're thinking you don't want to make an enemy, not this early. All right, Helen, I'll let this one slide but do keep an eye on Sandra. She's slack. And don't mention it to anyone else. Did you tick her off at least?'

'I did that.'

'Good. That's something.' Brian sipped his coffee.

Mavis wafted back through again, apparently oblivious to the both of them, their little nest of chairs, desk and computer.

'You know,' said Brian, 'she used to be the headmistress of a big posh private girls' school. Budgets, staffing, policies, curriculum, right on top of the whole show.'

His eyes followed Mavis up a corridor where he knew she would try another exit. And in a way he saw her naturally out in the dark, one with the dense community of ghost-gums forever pressing in on the home. Or perhaps haunting the 'highway' that Helen had referred to, Snake Gully Road, in some stretches scarcely wider than a path, one-way bitumen and gravel winding through the deserted foothills of Mount Wellington almost into Hobart itself. One of the original roads of the colony, Brian had read somewhere, probably an old Aboriginal trail. Other than the care workers here, who had to loop back onto it from streets lower down, Brian had never seen another driver use this road. The few dwellings strung out along it seemed to be deserted until you neared the city. The home had been built out here sometime in the 80s for cost and privacy. There was no one, nothing around for miles. The isolation also minimised visitors, those sons and daughters, husbands and wives, prompted by sorrow or guilt. That made life a bit easier. Brian would step outside for a break and relish the freshness and quiet, the smell of the forest, the sense of space. Yes, it was a pity the residents, such as Mavis Connell, couldn't also enjoy it.

Or Giles Patrick, presently strolling by, a gentleman flâneur in striped pyjamas, shrivelled cock peeking through his open flies. Giles did like to show his piece periodically, particularly to the female staff, but this looked inadvertent.

'Brian? You don't want to put them back to bed?'

'No point. They'll just get up again. Let them wear it out for a while.'

'Why do you think they do it? I mean, I know you think they're trying to get out but that couldn't be true for all of them. And why only at this time?'

'The sundowning, one of those many things that have never been adequately explained. Some think that when dementia patients get weary towards the end of the day, they get restless, others that a lack of sensory stimulation after dark cues disorientation. Truth is, nobody knows. Group behaviour is a funny thing. Like adolescent girls in boarding schools all having their periods together. Some kind of subliminal communication is going on. But yeah, you're right, I do think a lot of them are trying to get out. Why don't you ask Gwen here?'

Hearing her name, the resident immediately piped up. 'Can you tell me the time please?'

'Quarter to six, Gwen, my dear.'

With that mix of apathy and anxiety common to dementia, Gwen Alcott sat throughout the day, every day, on her special chair just outside the hub, watching the staff in whatever they did, periodically asking the time, nothing else. Brian smiled over at her but she gave no response. The left side of her face sagged from the stroke that had brought her into the home three years back. Maybe she couldn't smile, Brian thought, or it was difficult.

He reached into his pocket for a smoke, and realised for the umpteenth time that was all long finished. God, he could use one. In France, they had smoked everywhere. All these fucking do-gooders. Now they weren't even allowed to go outside for one. Geoff did, he knew, but as a supervisor he himself had to do the right thing.

'Helen, ever heard of a film called *The Sundowners*?'

'No.'

'Little before your time. Mine too. Sixties. Robert Mitchum, Deborah Kerr.'

'Never heard of them.'

'A sort of Aussie classic, well past its use-by date. Sheep drovers and shearers. Pitching their tent wherever the sun sets. I studied it at film school.'

'You wanted to make films?'

'Still do, sort of. The idea was that I would get some disposable job. Ten years on, I still haven't managed to dispose of it.'

'Did you make any?'

'A few shorts. Student stuff. After uni, I travelled to Europe and worked as an editor in France for a while. But I haven't kept up with the technology. I don't know. Difficult to let these dreams die. All those great ideas I had for films stacked up one after another in my head. Now they just seemed to have evaporated.'

'Maybe they'll come back to you.'

'Yeah, maybe. What I really should do is retrain and get a proper job. Get myself sorted.'

A scratching and shuffling from the ceiling.

'I've heard that before,' said Helen. 'Is it rats or birds, what?'

'That's Pete the possum. He's been here for as long as I have. You'll see him out near the bins. Beautiful creature. Thick glossy black pelt. Friendly too. This close to the bush we have to have a possum in residence. Can't avoid it. Occasionally, he comes into the home at night, looking for scraps, through some hole, we've never been able to find it.'

His buzzer: beep, beep, beep, beep… He clicked it off. 'Warranga Five. Bertie Benson. He probably needs toileting anyway.'

'Do you want me to get it?'

'It's my buzzer. Your turn next. You keep Gwen company.'

'Can you tell me the time please?'

'Six ten, Gwen.'

'Why don't you buy her a cheap watch?'

'Tried it. She destroys them.'

As Brian approached Bertie's room, evading the wafters, he could increasingly hear the man's loud incessant voice hammering like a machine:

'C'mon! C'mon! Four-four-five-five-hash! C'mon! C'mon! Six-two-three-two-hash!'

Jesus! He was reeling off the door codes! Brian entered the room, which stank of shit, to find the shrunken and intense Bertie in soiled tracksuit, neck thrust forward, head bobbing, pacing feverishly wall-to-wall reading from a laminated sheet held up inches from his eyes.

'Bertie, can I have that?'

'Hello, mate. Can you tell me the next bus to town?'

Bertie always asked this. 'Korsakoff Syndrome', alcohol-induced dementia, amongst other things. Always on edge, always wanting a fight – he'd been a pro boxer in his youth, occasionally self-harmed. All up he was pretty crazy, but also a lot like the drunks Brian had known when he worked bars as a student, same conversational tics, same matey bonhomie.

'Can you lend us ten bucks? Onto a sure thing at Elwick. You won't regret it, mate.'

'Bertie, please give me that sheet. Give me the sheet,Bertie.'

'Here you go, mate.'

'Thanks. Where did you get it?'

'From a mate. A sure thing.'

'Let's go into the bathroom and clean you up.'

'Sure thing, mate.'

Thank God at least for Helen. *La belle* Hélène. Definitely improved matters Still, it was going to be another long evening.

Next day, Thursday, Brian was on with Alan Burroughs for the same two to ten shift. Easy company. Brian arrived ten minutes early; as one of the two supervisors, along with Angela, it was important he made a show.

He accosted Sandra, the new girl, as she was leaving. 'Sandra, you know you're not meant to go until you're relieved.'

'I saw you coming. Angela said I could. My mum's been calling me non-stop.'

'What's wrong?'

'She's had a fall or something. Probably just drunk and rattled, but you never know.'

Sandra had recently taken in her mother who, from her accounts anyway, was more than a handful.

'Okay, there's something more serious. Did you have the door codes sheet out for any reason?'

'I was trying to learn them yesterday.'

Good, she'd told him the truth. 'Did you lock them back in the cupboard?'

'I can't remember. Maybe not.'

'I caught Bertie Benson with the codes last night. He's too scrambled to use them but if someone like James or Rufus got hold of them, we could be in trouble. James especially likes to make mischief. Those codes must be kept away from the residents. It's really important, Sandra. If they get out, for any reason, it's a big deal. Understood?'

'Sure. I'm sorry, Brian.'

'Try and think, okay? Now because I caught Bernie with them, I'm going to have to write an incident report. You don't want too many of those with your name on them.'

'Brian, I've really got to go.'

'Did you hear what I said?'

'Yes, a report. I said I'm sorry.'

'All right. I hope your mum's fine.'

She brushed past him. Alan had passed them both on the path. Brian clocked in and told him and Angela about the breach.

Alan shrugged as his buzzer went off. 'No rest for the wicked,' he said. He put his bag in his locker and walked off.

'How has the shift gone, Ang?'

'No big problems. James is a headache.'

'What's new? He's got it in for you for some reason. I don't know. You're just going to have to deal with it until it goes away.'

'If it does.'

'He'll wear it out, then find something else. Or someone. When I first came here, James kept telling everyone I was gay, even though he knew I wasn't. If I protested, I'd look homophobic. It's these mind games he likes to play. Go home and try and forget about it.' His buzzer. James. He held it up to Angela. 'Speak of the devil.'

'He's after me.'

'He's out of luck. Go home.'

Brian dumped his gear and made his way down to James's door. Knocked.

'Come in.'

James was perched in front of his computer, as per usual, playing solitaire. He swung around on his automated wheelchair, eyeing Brian coldly. 'And where's our lovely Miss Angela?'

'Finished her shift. What do you want, James?'

'I need someone to put me on the toilet. Number two.'

He drove into the bathroom and Brian helped him get comfortable.

'I'll call you when I finish. Hang around. I won't be long.'

Brian closed the door and glanced around. James's room looked neat and tidy. Brian looked at the screen for a while with the cards, then he minimised it and brought up James's files. A lot of games, some porn, what was this? 'Codes'. He opened it. The door codes. Shit! It was dated yesterday. James must have picked up the sheet, transcribed it, and then passed it to Bertie. Why didn't he put it back where he found it? Because he knew someone would find Bertie with it and that would spook them all. Typical. Brian deleted the file. It was unlikely there'd be a back-up. And James wouldn't have had time to learn it. He hoped. What to do? Say nothing. James would see the file gone and that would be an end to it. Of course, residents' files were meant to be private, but the man could hardly complain about this.

Back at the nurses' station, Brian boiled up the jug for himself and Alan. 'Let's hope for a quiet one. Can you work a double shift with me? Sandra's texted that her mum needs support and the casual's called in sick.'

'No problem.'

Nothing seemed too much of a problem for Alan, which from Brian's point of view, in this job, was a godsend. Alan was a bachelor in his forties, laid-back, unflustered but also efficient. Brian had long given up wondering what made the man tick. Probably made more sense pondering why he himself expected more than life was prepared to deliver. Brian looked him over: small and neat, short-back-and-sides, always well-groomed. The only one of them who never wore jeans. He was flicking through the care plans on the hub's computer.

'Looking for anything?'

'Just making sure they're up to date. Consistent, whatever.'

Although he looked like an accountant, Alan had told Brian about how he had fronted a heavy metal band back in the early nineties, Hatchet. Local, but did some mainland touring, the festivals circuit and a few backups for big acts. And a couple of albums. So, quite successful. A bass guitarist and vocalist, he still played around the pub scene with different bands. Brian couldn't imagine him with groupies and drugs. Maybe he'd changed his style, maybe it was a Jekyll-and-Hyde thing.

'Brian, I thought I should tell you that I've had more complaints than usual from residents about not getting to sleep.'

'They don't do anything all day.'

'Most of them have sleeping tablets in the Webster packs. Bertie's got enough to fell an elephant.'

'Bertie's wired.'

'Sure, but Ben also, who's not wired at all. Quite the opposite.'

'We give them out,' said Brian.

'But maybe we're not watching them closely enough as they take them. Or some of us aren't.'

'Maybe, but then why would residents not take their sleeping tabs?'

'I don't know. Yeah, I guess it doesn't make sense.' He looked up from the computer. 'Must be something else.'

'What's bugging you?'

'Not sure.'

'Okay, Alan, I'll send a text message around confirming procedure, that all staff make doubly sure that the residents take all their meds. Monitor them as they should. I mean, this is standard stuff. We write them up and everything.'

'Still, if people are slack. No names...' He shrugged.

Happy Valley Nursing Home, a lockdown round-the-clock care facility, privately owned, forty high maintenance residents, mostly dementia with a few disabled, with two staff in attendance at any one time. There were two nurses, an RN and EN, Angela and Helen, both on call, and two supervisors, Brian and, again, Angela. There was a cook, Josie, who came in to assist with the evening meal, but otherwise the rotating staff of six: Brian, Helen, Sandra, Angela, Alan and Geoff, along with some casuals, did all the cleaning and kitchen work and laundry. Helen and Sandra were new, and Angela was relatively new, but the three men had worked at the home for years. The resident population also was relatively stable, a couple of deaths per annum amongst the older ones, readily replaced. It was basic, but it was functional, so thought Brian, who had been there the longest.

Sometime after midnight, Brian did a full round and poked his head in all the doors, and it did seem, as Alan had said, that most of the clients were awake, either on their computers or watching TV or just staring at the ceiling in the dark. It was a little strange, but he couldn't see anything sinister in it. Like the sundowning, occasionally it happened that odd herd behavioural phenomena would sweep the home for no apparent reason.

Next morning, Friday, Angela had the six-to-two shift with Sandra, who'd come in to make up for missing the overnighter. Brian and Alan had worked sixteen hours straight.

'You okay?' Angela asked Brian.

'Yeah, I grabbed a few hours in the early morning. Alan had everything under control. Nothing much to report, you can read the notes, except the residents don't seem to be sleeping much.'

'Since the middle of last week. I was going to mention it. Don't know why. But no one seems fussed except Bertie. These things happen. I guess they'll start sleeping shortly.'

'So will I.'

'Six tomorrow morning with Helen, yes?'

'I'll be here.'

The six a.m. to two p.m. shift was a busy one because it included two meals. Brian and Alan had already prepared the breakfast plates of fruit and cereal and sandwiches, and itemised them. Angela and Sandra split up the residents.

'Sandra, do you mind doing James?'

She winced. 'Ang, he's already specifically asked for you. Said he wouldn't eat either of his meals unless you brought them.'

'How did he even know I was on shift?'

'James seems to know everything.'

'All right. I'll get him out of the way first up.'

She retrieved James's breakfast from the fridge. It was the same as his lunch, same as always – white bread and cheddar cheese slices, four little triangles with the crusts removed, plus an orange juice. His meds were not due till ten. Sandra could do them. As Angela approached his room, she recalled the mantra from her training, that with difficult residents it was important to normalise the relationship as quickly as possible, not avoid them. Not allow them to believe they were manipulating you.

She slipped on plastic gloves from the dispenser on the wall, knocked on his door and he growled, 'Come in.'

When he saw, it was her, the customary smirk appeared. 'Our lovely Miss Angela. My lucky day. Come to give me a morning hand job?'

She must ignore it. 'I've brought breakfast.'

He was up and dressed. At least Brian had done that for her. James swung his wheelchair away from the computer (she was always surprised how fluently he controlled it), leaving the card game on hold, and over to the bed. He looked at her coldly, but still smirking. Whenever she saw James, Angela always had this funny idea she'd seen him before somewhere, although she knew that couldn't be right.

'Sit on the bed next to me. You're a natural for the bed.'

Ignore that too.

'Would you like a drink or a sandwich first?'

He could operate the computer and his chair with his hands, but for some reason could not lift them.

'Sandwich.'

'White bread and cheese. You always have the same thing. Don't you ever want something else?'

'It doesn't matter. All food is bitter to me, my dear.'

This was one of these slightly odd statements that James was always making. Angela never knew quite how to respond to them. She placed one of the triangles in his open mouth and he jerked his head forward and bit down on her forefinger and held it between his teeth. She waited. He kept his grip and looked up at her, smirk increasing.

'Come on, James. What do you expect me to do?'

He moved his tongue around her finger. She said nothing and waited.

Finally, he released her and chewed and swallowed. 'It's a pity about the glove. I'm sure you're tastier than this cheese. Tell me, my lovely Angela, do you like pain? Under certain circumstances? I understand some women do.'

James spoke with a beautifully polished accent. Angela found the sound of it alone honeyed and seductive, even with its sardonic edge. She picked up another sandwich and placed it in his mouth, withdrawing her hand quickly.

He smiled at her discomfort. 'You don't trust me. You think I want to hurt you? There are some in this place who would love to hurt you.'

'Why do you say that? I don't bear anyone ill will.'

'Of course. That's part of the provocation. Such a desirable woman.'

'I'm ordinary, as you know.' Plain Jane, her mother had always called her. Still, men had always noticed her body. Those side glances.

'You're desirable to me. Eye of the beholder.'

'Now Helen, James, she's pretty.' Angela, overly tall, thought of Helen as like a little doll, with her short-cropped black hair and babyish face.

'That Scottish tart. Big bold Brian, our forlorn Fellini, is drooling all over her like some child molester. Have you noticed?'

'Not really.'

'Beauty's a funny thing. You can't really do anything with it, except destroy it.' He paused, presumably to let this oddity sink in.

A scratching above; they both glanced up to the ceiling.

'It's that fucking possum. You should kill it.'

'They're protected, I think. Another one would just replace it. Anyway, it's a sin to take life for no reason.'

'It's just a pest. A sin to take life. Cokehead Geoff told me that after high school you entered orders, wanted to become a nun. Is that true?'

'Many years back.'

'What happened?'

'Why didn't I become a nun? I didn't have the commitment.'

'You would have had to give up sex. No more fucking for the rest of your life. So, do you still believe in God?'

'Yes, of course.'

'You know my parents were religious. They told me I was a gift from God, a cripple like me, can you believe that?'

'Don't refer to yourself like that, James.'

'Why not? It's how the world views me. Disabled, differently abled: all that's nonsense. I'm a cripple, Angela. A cripple. Say it!'

'No!'

'A child sees me in the street. What does it see? A disturbing mixture of the grotesque and the familiar that I so naturally embody. Like a bad fairy tale. "Don't look at him like that," says mother, trying to pull the child away, but the child doesn't want to go, the child is both fascinated and repulsed. Trying to work me out, fit me in. Fascination and repulsion. I believe that's the way a woman looks at a man's genitals. What do you think?'

'Look, James, I have other residents to attend to. Do you want another sandwich?'

'A man's most bestial part. And you also, Angela, you must have felt loathing and perhaps even horror the first time you saw a seriously disabled individual, a real live cripple like me.'

'Have you finished?'

'I'm just getting started. There is a television placed in my room so that I can connect to the real world, but that real world bears no relation to the reality of my experience. It mocks me, Angela, with all its normal people. Even more, the world excludes me from its reality. It puts me out here in the bush, all of us, so the world doesn't have to see us. Out of sight, out of mind. But I am here nevertheless. God didn't finish me properly so I have finished myself, in my own way, in Happy Valley Nursing Home. A gift of God. Fucking hell! Your stupid training tells you all to help me strive beyond my disabilities, to become as normal as possible. What you miss is that my disabilities define me. I am who I am because of what I am.'

'James, listen to me. We are all gifts of God.'

'Don't repeat their horseshit! Every Sunday off, we went to church. La-de-da. I swallowed it for a while until I realised what life, I mean your God, had dealt me.'

'You don't believe any more.'

He didn't answer.

'Are your parents still alive?' She couldn't recall anyone visiting him.

'No. Small mercy. They never wanted me anyway. Best gone.'

He leant forward slightly to take another sandwich. Angela popped it in quickly, again betraying her fear of being bitten and again his amusement at this, but while he was chewing, the smirk left his face, to be replaced by a sort of indrawn seriousness.

He swallowed and faced her directly, his eyes glittering. 'I don't believe in God, but I do hate Him.'

'That doesn't make sense.'

'Polio, before I could even talk. Did you know?'

'Yes.'

'You've read my case notes. Good girl. Why did it strike me?'

'No reason.'

'Your God gave me polio.'

Angela was reminded of a description of onset polio in her course work as a 'silver tingling', which had made it sound almost like a spiritual experience. From his notes, James had nearly died. He had the torso and head of a grown man, but little shrivelled useless legs. His arms were also small, with limited mobility. His head, perhaps in comparison, seemed unusually large, bald and bony with a prominent jawline and piercing blue eyes. Angela imagined he would have been tall and strong if not for the disease.

'Why should you be whole and not me?' He watched her steadily without blinking.

'I don't know.'

'I've never been out of a wheelchair. Imagine. Never made love to a woman. Never been able to have a job. There's your God. Fuck your God. Fuck you too.'

Angela took a deep breath, recomposed herself. Then, without a further word, she fed him the last sandwich, gave him his juice and left.

James returned to his game but it bored him. He switched to porn but then after a few minutes he became angry and turned off the computer. He wheeled over to a patch of sunlight to calm himself. He could never watch porn after Angela, although he always felt he wanted to. He'd noted that someone had deleted the door codes file, no doubt Brian. But then he'd already sent a copy to Rufus, who now would know them by heart. Rufus was a like a computer himself. Very like. So, yes, it was finally starting.

The following morning, Saturday. Brian and Helen were preparing the breakfasts the two overnight casuals had characteristically neglected.

'Do they pasteurise the milk in Scotland?'

'Think so. I'm a city girl.'

'They don't in France. Because of the cheese industry. And so the cheese is fabulous.'

'Where did you work in France?'

'Lyon. Lovely city, famous for its food, well, the food's good all over France. But after a while I got homesick and came back. Now I wish I hadn't.' Brian was also thinking how he'd left a daughter in Lyon. Angelique. He kept in touch with Jacquie, even though she'd partnered up again. Yes, turning twelve this year, cusp of womanhood. He'd have to get back over some time. Unfinished business.

'Helen, you must have been to France.'

'School excursion to Paris for four days. I come from a big family.

There wasn't any money for travelling or anything like that. I haven't even been to London that much.'

'Why did you come all the way down to Tasmania?'

'I don't know. Sounded exotic.'

'Exotic! Jesus!'

'Hobart's nice. I'd like to stay. Maybe do some more study and become an RN. I think I could make a good life for myself here.'

With some lucky bugger, thought Brian. He'd always been attracted to small women. Neat, petite and sweet. Wanted to protect them, probably. He himself was big and gangly, still okay for early thirties, no gut, bit of a widow's peak. Hadn't had anything to do with a woman in over a year. Probably a decade plus between him and Helen. Surely, she'd be out for younger game, but then who knows?

'Do you want James or Rufus?' he asked.

'Doesn't matter. They don't give me any problems.'

'They must be saving you up. I'll take James.'

Helen picked up Rufus's tray, toast spread with Nutella and a glass of Coke, the only things he would eat and drink, and headed down to his room. She could hear his video game well in advance, the roar and crackle. He played the one game only: Pyro, a fantasy aimed at teenage boys who were firebugs. She donned her gloves, knocked, no answer, Rufus never answered, and backed in with the tray.

'Morning, Rufus! Breakfast!'

Still no response. He was bolted to his screen as per usual. Rufus was autistic, no social skills, no facial expressions, no eye contact, minimal speech, but unlike other autistic residents Helen had worked with, he was highly functional in certain ways. He had an extraordinary memory, knew all the staff's and residents' birthdays, dates of all kinds, sports scores, historical trivia, seemingly everything he had come across in his life, and commanded this complicated game which he played all day and well into the night, effortlessly accumulating bonus points for further screen time. Like a big kid. He looked like a big kid too with his unkempt hair and thick black plastic square glasses, presently reflecting flashes from the screen which also cast his immobile face in shifting un-earthly glows. Except that he wasn't a kid, he was a man in his mid-thir-ties, difficult and unreachable.

Rufus had come to Happy Valley as a reject from a succession of homes, each one of which he had tried to set alight. Heedless of his own safety and that of other residents, he would light fires in his room, garbage tins, kitchens, rec rooms, anywhere. He was also addicted to video games. Brian had described to Helen how, when Rufus arrived, on an inspiration he had searched through numerous games until he came across Pyro. He introduced it to an ecstatic Rufus and, so far at least, there had hardly been any incidents. Miraculously, it seemed, for the present Rufus had transferred his obsession from the real world to fantasy, where it could do little harm. Still, it was an unstable situation, and the staff and Brian particularly were always aware of Rufus's destructive potential.

Helen came around the back of his chair and placed the breakfast tray next to the keyboard. Still no acknowledgement. He was wearing a black tracksuit. She wasn't sure whether he had changed into it or had slept in it. Probably the latter. He smelt. It was notoriously difficult to get Rufus to change his clothes or wash. But that was Brian's problem. When he got hungry, he would pick at the food. She would check in later to make sure he had eaten some of it. She did a quick scan of his room and bathroom, both of which seemed in reasonable order. Then she left him to it and returned to the kitchen.

Ben was next on her list. A simple soul, totally complaisant. His case notes told a story how four years back, a woman claiming to be his aunt came with Ben to the Home to investigate the possibility of placing him there. She put Ben in the toilet, then asked Brian whether she could have a quick look at the surrounds. Brian let her out and she drove off. Ben had no identification of any kind on him, and the staff had no way of contacting this 'aunt'. Ben knew nothing, could barely speak or remember. There was not a thing to go on. Brian had made the usual inquiries but Ben, if that really was his name, seemed to be-long to no one and nowhere.

So he became a ward of the state and a permanent resident of the home. He seemed barely sentient, spoke only when spoken to, was not interested in television or computer games, just sat in his room quietly, looking out his large picture window at the bush and the birds as though he would like to join them. He did everything that was asked of him and never caused any trouble.

'Good morning, Ben.'

He was up, dressed, and sitting in his chair. He turned to present to her his perfectly calm, bland face.

'Would you like some breakfast?'

'Yes.'

Helen wheeled a portable table around in front of him and placed his tray down and he at once started to eat. She had brought his meds from the storage cabinet, three digestives for each meal and a sleeping tab for the night. She pressed out the digestive and watched him swallow it. He held out his hand.

'What do you want, Ben?'

'My sleeping pill.'

'That's not due till tonight.'

'Can I have it now?'

'No. Why?'

'James wants them.'

'Sorry?'

'James wants them.'

'They're not for James. They're for you. Only you. Do you understand?'

'Yes.'

When Helen had finished with Ben, she reported the exchange to Brian. Brian then confronted James. Mock innocent denials. Plus smirks.

'James told me he just asked Ben the one time, when he was having trouble sleeping, if Ben could somehow save a pill for him. Ben must have put it in his mouth and not swallowed it or something.'

'Or just kept it in his hand. I don't think it would be too difficult to get something like that past Sandra, for example.'

'But something like what? James let me search his rooms. I couldn't find anything. I can't imagine why he'd want to stockpile them, if that's what he's doing.'

'Then maybe he's telling the truth. He just wanted the one.'

'He could have come to us if he wanted an extra. I don't know.'

'Can you tell me the time please?'

Helen smiled. 'Seven thirty, Gwen. Have you had your breakfast?'

'I gave it to her first up. She's always keen to get out here on duty.' Brian creased his brow. 'I've never trusted James. I just don't know.'

Next morning, Sunday six to two, Geoff and Sandra. Examining his stubble above the mirror in the staff toilet, Geoff Colvin, twenty-eight, bit of a lad, never found the time to organise a proper career, but not unhappy with Happy Valley. There were worse jobs; he'd done plenty. He'd done plenty last night too, standard Saturday binge, early shift notwithstanding. Mostly booze, the old gang, also lads, dead-end jobs, no girlfriends, who cares. Four thirty he took an Uber home, showered, changed, couldn't handle breakfast, popped his last speed pill to tide him through. A good decision, he was still feeling functional, although by early afternoon he'd be a right piece of shit. It didn't matter. With the new girl, Sandra, the other new girl, not that Scottish nurse Brian was keeping to himself, jigging the roster. Well, he's the boss. Didn't bug Geoff, but back at the hub it was bugging Sandra.

'The two of them, Brian and Angela, they just suit themselves.'

'As supervisors do. Why would you want to be on a shift with Helen? And what's Angela done?

'She never has a Sunday morning shift. Off to church, the ex-nun.'

'Her belief, it's a personal thing. You gotta respect it.'

'Don't see why. Had a rare Saturday night planned. Hens' night. I never get out at all what with Mum as she is, but I doped her with two of those pills you gave me.'

'So why didn't you go? No way an early shift would stop me. I haven't slept a wink.'

'I did go, but I had to be home by ten when things were just warming up. I need at least six hours or I can't cope.'

'You youngsters haven't any stamina. Listen, just go easy on those pills. They're the residents'. They're pretty strong.'

'You nicked the residents' pills?'

'They'd already been nicked. Buggered if I know how. I found a stash in one of Rufus's drawers. Well, five or so. I thought they were just Rufus's and he hadn't taken them because he was wanting to play his fire-shit all night or something. So I ticked him off and pocketed them so I wouldn't have to write a report, then, per Brian's text, it turns out all the residents have been avoiding taking them and then handing them over, when they could, to someone for some reason. James was mentioned but he hasn't got them. Who knows what's going on? Anyway, now Brian's onto it, it will stop.'

'James tried to finger you. He told me you'd probably taken them because you'd taken codeine from the security locker in the past.'

'Yeah, well, that was years ago. I was going through a bad patch. Brian found me out and read the riot act. I've been a good boy since. Don't go talking about it, though. Brian gave me a break. It's a sackable offence, nicking pills. So don't mention the sleeping tabs either. I mean, you asked me 'cause of your mum. I was doing you a favour.'

'I know, Geoff, I know. Don't worry.' Her buzzer rang. 'Shit, it's Joyce! Why do I always get her? Do you mind, Geoff? I can't deal with her, really.'

'She gives you a harder time because you're new. Standard stuff. She thinks she can freak you out.'

'She's not wrong.'

'Okay, I'll get her, but you've got to learn to handle the difficult ones, Sandra, if you want to stay in the job. I'll see what she wants but next time she buzzes, if it's your turn, you take it.'

'All right, all right.'

As he walked towards her room, Geoff forced his scattered thoughts into focus and brought Joyce and her condition to mind. Joyce had an inoperable tumour in the frontal lobe of her brain, the area concerned with personality and emotions. She was thirty-five. Six years ago, she was running a successful physiotherapy practice in Main Street, Moonah. Geoff had actually once seen her for a strained tendon from jogging, back when he used to exercise. She had been courteous and professional, warm and helpful, and had fixed him up quick smart.

And now this: utterly changed, unrecognisable, a wild obscene harridan, constantly demanding cigarettes, abusing staff and residents day and night. By this point, all her relatives and friends had given up, even the immediate family. In a few years, she would be dead but until then Happy Valley staff had to deal with her. He met her halfway up her corridor.

'I want the new bitch, mate. She around?'

'My name's Geoff. See the tag? Sandra's in the loo. What do you want, Joyce?'

'A smoke.'

'Can't help you. Sorry.'

'Bullshit. I know you sneak them like Brian.'

'No one's allowed cigarettes any more. You know.'

'Listen, you give me one of your fucking smokes or I'll tell Brian you've been perving at me in the shower.'

'I don't have any.'

'James says he sees you smoking outside. James says you nick codeine from the meds cupboard.'

'James says anything that suits him.'

'I'll tell Brian that too.'

Maybe someone else had been nicking codeine. Nah, it was all crap. Since his little indiscretion, Brian policed the meds cupboard like a hawk, particularly the schedule eights, the heavy proscribed stuff. And back whenever, Brian had known who it was because he did all the pharmacy orders and purchases and put two and two together with the shifts. Brian didn't want him sacked, because, whatever Geoff did out-side work, he was reliable and efficient and never missed a shift and they'd worked together for years. Anyway, it was always only ever for personal use. And for the overnighters, sometimes he just had to be wired, which no doubt James was sensitive to, like he was to everything. But these days, he always sourced the stuff from outside.

'You tell him, Joyce.'

'You wanna fuck me?'

'No, Joyce.'

'You a fucking pooftah? As if I'd want your miserable prick! What a joke!' She went off cackling down the corridor, hopefully back to her room.

Well, it was shaping up to be one of those days. A bit of codeine on top of the speed would actually smooth him out nicely. He dug in the fog pocket of his jeans and found a foiled tab from the previous evening. Thought he'd done them all but you never know your luck. He made his way back to the hub.

'How was our Joyce?'

'Pretty much as usual.' He looked at the schedule. 'You want to give Joan Fallows a shower? She would have finished her breakfast by now.'

'No worries.'

Geoff waited a minute or two, then listened outside Joan Fallows's door until he could hear the water running, and then made his way over to the entrance lobby to the staff lockers. He unlocked his and pulled out an old hippy bag of woven yak's wool brought back from Nepal a decade ago. It was in Nepal and then India that he'd picked up his drug habit which, really, had been far worse going back a few years. He fished out a small flask of Napoleon brandy and washed down the powder with a couple of big glugs. Then popped a peppermint in his mouth to mask the alcohol, not that Sandra was likely to notice, or care. He started to feel better already, just anticipating the charge.

Sandra sat outside the open shower curtain watching Joan Fallows clumsily soap herself with a sponge. She was fine, just needed a watchful eye in case she lost her balance. After the wash, Sandra did her feet. Almost all the elderly residents seemed to have trouble with their feet, the most common culprit being, as in Joan's case, diabetes. Fortunately, Sandra didn't have to deal with any sores; that was for the nurses, Angela and Helen. Joan's feet and lower legs were okay at present, despite being an unhealthy purple and swollen with oedema, so just some eucalyptus oil between the toes and a careful massage with a zinc moisturiser. Joan sighed at her attentions. Pain or pleasure? Would she herself ever have legs like this? One day, probably. Hard to imagine, growing old, being old. In her mind, various possibilities yet unrealised stretched away into a hazy distance. Death was so far off she never even thought of it. But Joan must think of it.

She shouldn't have mentioned the pills to Geoff. He was doing her a favour, as he said. She liked Geoff. He was the best person to be on shift with because he was always juiced up in some way and so did most of the work. Even without the chemicals, she suspected he was just one of those hyperactive guys. Sharp face, afro hair, skinny as shit. Unlike herself, to put it mildly.

Sandra Levitt always worried people would see her as fat, when really she wasn't, just big-boned with a generous covering. Her last boyfriend had actually tried to stop her dieting, said he preferred her with a bit of flesh. She remembered it fondly. He'd taken a job in Melbourne and she hadn't followed him there out of sheer inertia, which was the second way that she differed from Geoff. Sandra was one of those naturally phlegmatic souls, happiest when doing nothing at all. Any chore was a bore, always had been. That extended to personal hygiene.

Not that the guys cared if you wore the same clothes as per the last shift and hadn't washed in a while. Helen and Angela noticed, though, and Angela had ticked her off. Angela was onto her, knew she was lazy, so when around her, sharing duties or whatever, Sandra had to make sure she stepped up to the mark. She didn't want to lose this job. It was reasonably easy work, if sometimes a bit yucky, and all routine, which suited her. Just the nuisance of the variable shifts, although you did have to avoid the nasties like Joyce or James, or the crazies like Bertie. But with Mum now at home to watch over, there was no more slacking on the dole. It was good she could knock her off from time to time with these pills from Geoff, while they lasted. Long term, she didn't know what to do about her mother. She could apply for a carer's wage but then she'd be stuck at home all the time with her.

When her mother's last 'boyfriend' – that is, root/scrounger – had vamoosed with her computer and stereo and a few other items, she just terminated her lease and moved in with Sandra. That was six months back. Her mother was depressed, she said, correct diagnosis, either in bed awake and moaning, or in front of Sandra's telly watching daytime free-to-air which would depress anyone. Fortunately, she was on sickness benefits wangled from some doctor but she seemed to spend most of it on cigarettes and booze, despite being a type B diabetic. Hopefully in time she'd just get bored and move on, find herself another root/scrounger, but for the present she seemed pretty settled. Sandra would wait it out. Her general theory of living was that if you did nothing, eventually the world left you alone. It hadn't proved to be right thus far, but she was in it for the long haul. She knew what she wanted from life: minimal this, minimal that. Eventually, she'd work herself into the right situation.

Angela and Alan relieved for the two-to-ten. At the hub, Alan boiled up the jug for both of them. This was always an easy shift to start off with. He could ease into it, morning showers done, just making sure lunch had been eaten and meds taken, bit of cleaning up, the usual load of washing, and prep for the evening meal, which the regular staff had to cook on a Sunday. But the clients always threw something new at you and also there was the sundowning after dinner when half the home was on the loose and you had to be up to their tricks.

But nothing to get too excited about. That's all he wanted these days, so different to when he was young. Those days, he was excited about everything, particularly since he was going to be a big rock star.

But then after some years of strive and stress, he realised he wasn't going to be a big rock star. Still, being a muso was what he loved, Hobart had a great pub band scene, so what he needed was to find some kind of steady support job he could work around his various gigs. And after a few false starts, this was it. Like with the bands, he'd do this until he couldn't do it any longer. No marriage, no property. His parents thought he had never grown up which, depending on how you viewed it, might be true, but he was fine doing what he was doing so who gave a shit?

He just had to avoid too much drugs and booze, always a temptation on the scene, look after himself, and in fact, middle-age, he was still pulling in the odd bird. He'd taken home a medical student last night after they'd played the final set. It was her one night off in three weeks and she seemed determined to score. So he nominated himself. No big problem getting it up, you were never quite sure these days, but then she was pretty helpful, knew her anatomy, and was grateful for him cooking her breakfast too. Smiles all round.

He poured out the teas. 'Here you go, Ang.'

Angela was a good shift co-worker, experienced and diligent. It didn't fuss Alan she was over a decade younger and his superior. Five years ago, he'd been offered a supervisor's position and knocked it back. Brian got it. Brian was more suited, plus Alan thought the extra money just wasn't worth the hassle. Angela seemed a bit on edge today. He guessed she'd gone to church, maybe that was it, although why would it be?

'Listen, Ang, if James buzzes, I'll do it, no worries.' He knew how much James upset her. James was such a pain in the fucking arse.

'No, thanks, Alan, really, I've got to learn to deal with him.'

'As you like. But the offer holds.'

'Can you tell me the time please?'

'Two thirty, Gwen.'

Angela was on edge, and it was attending Mass that had done it. These days, she felt like a hypocrite, although she knew she wasn't. She genuinely believed in God and the Catholic faith, even if she hadn't been up to being a nun. Of course, you could be devout and sincere and not be a nun, like most worshippers. The problem was certain things she could not stop herself thinking about, which God would be aware of. It wasn't only the petty and mean-minded – she assumed almost everybody had these thoughts from time to time – but glancing around at the parishioners this morning, she couldn't credit that these people, heads quietly bowed, had the type and degree of erotic imaginings she seemed to have had since the age of fourteen, that she had never been able to prevent and she knew God must disapprove of. As did she. And even though she knew God knew these things, she had also never been able to confess them.

If Angela Jackson had had to describe herself, the first word that would've come to mind would be 'idealist', and the second 'sensualist'. The two made an uneasy fit. During her late adolescence, her religious faith had become an obsession for her and, looking back, she saw that it probably contained an erotic element in its extremity. Her family were devout Catholics, but even they had baulked at her 'calling' to be a nun, although in some ways it was an extension of her schooling. She would enter orders and then become a nurse. Well, she had done both of those things but had not lasted long with the sisters. It had nothing to do with any crisis of faith. She had always believed and would all her life; faith was central to her sense of being.

The problem had been her libido, which had reached a sort of a 'mania' during her time in orders. She had had a number of relationships since then, but each of them had been largely driven by sex and ultimately unsuccessful. Throwing off the burden of virginity seemed to have increased her drive rather than slaked it. And in fact, the reason she was in this present job was partly as an escape from a specific sexual dilemma.

At the previous home Angela had worked, there had been a boy – a young man – who she had once known: Cody. As a schoolgirl, she'd watched him while waiting for her bus at the Glenorchy bus mall. He always hung around there with a bunch of thugs, his mates, smoking, swearing, drinking, but unlike them, he was beautiful, an angel acting like a devil. She had never spoken to him of course, that would have been impossible, and he would never have been interested in her anyway when he could have his pick of all the pretty girls. She had forgotten about him over the years, first in the convent, then at uni, and suddenly here he was again. He had been hit by a bus when drunk late one night and now he had no use of limbs and no cognition. He mumbled to himself and only occasionally could words be distinguished.

Cody still had urinary function and instead of the usual tube had a device called a uridome fitted onto his penis which was connected to a bag. Each morning, it would need to be refitted. Curiously, not only was Cody's urinary function unimpaired but also his sexual function. So also each morning, like any healthy young man, he would wake with an erection and the carers would need to wait until it subsided for the new uridome to be fitted. Each morning when the sheets were stripped back, his penis erect against his stomach, Cody would mumble, 'Get on me, get on me.' He had a long lean body, not a shred of fat, the almost unnaturally creamy glow of his skin highlighted by a blue tattoo patterning one tightly muscled flank. 'Get on me, get on me,' he would murmur and each morning Angela had to deal with him, that was exactly what she wanted to do.

While the other carer folded fresh clothes in the corner or busied themselves with some other task waiting until Cody was flaccid, Angela would surreptitiously watch him, just as she had done at the bus mall, and fantasise hiking her skirts or taking off her jeans, kneeling astride him exposed on the bed and taking his penis in her hand. As soon as she did so, she imagined he would suddenly come back to full conscious life, galvanised, like a miracle from Jesus, the mischievous dangerous Cody, up to no good, he would look straight through her with his cheeky smile, know her persistent desire, and cupping his strong fine hands under her buttocks, gently parting them, would ease her down onto him.

This fantasy continually haunted her while she worked. She was ashamed of it, sick of it, she was just like a dirty boy, but she eventually found that the only way she was able to put it to rest was by leaving that home and coming to this one. Yes, some nun she would have made. Imagine the sisters thinking of something like that!

Her buzzer.

'It's James,' she sighed.

'Are you sure?'

'I'll get it, Alan. I mean, I'm meant to be a supervisor and all!'

She gave herself a moment outside his door before knocking. 'Afternoon, James. What's up?'

'I've been missing you. I'm feeling a little stiff. What about a massage? I'll direct you.'

'Have you finished your lunch?'

'Did you hear me? You asked what's up. I've been reading online about these sexual therapists. Have you heard of them?'

'Yes.'

'You should consider it.'

'I think it's a type of prostitution.'

'That's just your conservative Catholic prejudice. Anyway, "Sex worker" is the term these days. I thought you knew all your terms. Did you go to church this morning?'

'Yes.'

'Tell me, Angela, do you ever sense the Devil in church? Do you?'

'That's a personal question.'

'Is it now? Personal. Interesting. What if you were to find out that, for example, I was a devil?'

'You told me that you don't believe in God. You can't be a devil if you don't believe in God.'

'Clever girl. But you believe in God. I might be a devil to you. I could become your devil. A devil is half bestial, just like me. I don't have proper legs and feet. Look a little more closely, my lovely. There might really be horns and hooves.'

'Don't be silly.'

'Familiarity breeds contempt. You see me every day and so you cannot see what I really am.'

'Enough, James. Now, really, is there anything you need me to do for you.'

'Oh, many things.'

'Look, there's a list of duties outside waiting for me.'

'All right, I'll let you go. But I'll call you back later. The Devil's always calling, Angela.'

She collected his lunch tray and left. Even this little exchange with James left her frazzled and she had an eight-hour shift ahead.

Ten-to-six, the overnighter into Monday morning, was Brian and Sandra. This was Sandra's favourite shift, where you basically just had to stay awake and occasionally assist clients to the toilet and readjust their sleeping positions. In the morning, there were the breakfast preps. She didn't mind staying up. She'd had a nap in the afternoon and knocked her Mum out with another one of Geoff's pills, and no one cared on the overnighters if you goofed off reading magazines or whatever. She could happily sit around for hours completely absorbed in her own thoughts.

Brian used the overnighters for catching up on online 'paperwork' and checking all the registers and stocks. He thought he'd also try and find some minor tasks for Sandra to do, make her earn her keep.

It was three in the morning, Brian was sitting at the hub computer with a mug of coffee setting the upcoming rosters when Sandra's scream, recognisably Sandra's, pierced the fuggy night air. Brian hurried to the sound. Sandra was standing frozen in a dimly lit corridor wordlessly pointing at Joyce, stark naked, with a long kitchen knife in one hand, and in the other, outstretched, the tail of, it had to be, Pete the possum, twitching a little, gut slit wide open, from which oozed purple viscera and blood and some kind of yellow fluid. There was a terrible stink. Of flesh and of fear.

'Fucking fucking pest! James told me. Kill it, Joyce! Fucking pest!'

Brian approached cautiously. 'Give me the knife, Joyce.'

'Pete the pest!' she cackled wildly.

'You can keep Pete. Just give me the knife.'

'Keep this fucking pest? You keep it!' She swung the animal around and let it fly off in the general direction of Brian and Sandra.

While her eyes followed the possum, Brian lunged at her and grabbed her right wrist. She tried to transfer the knife to her other hand but he was too quick, wrenching it from her and hurling it towards Sandra.

'You get your fucking hands off me. I'm naked. You could be in big trouble.'

'Sandra, give us a hand here, will you.'

Sandra reluctantly helped him wrestle Joyce back to her room. Brian deftly pushed her inside, he'd obviously done this with residents before, and locked her in using the outside safety latch. They could hear her cackling away. Fortunately, she wasn't enraged, which meant, Brian hoped, that she would probably calm down in time, and maybe even forget about what she'd done and put herself back to bed. Brian saw Sandra was pretty shaken. Little wonder. They were both panting.

'You okay?'

'Not really. She was incredibly strong. I mean you're a man and I'm much bigger than her.'

'Yeah. I don't think she was intending to use the knife against us.'

'How do you know?'

'Look, you clean the knife and lock all the kitchen drawers. I'll deal with the possum and the stain on the carpet. We'll have to keep all the drawers locked from now on. We really should have been doing it all along but no one's ever taken a knife before, or anything. I'll send around a text and add a note to the procedures book. Then we'll both sit down and write an incident report.'

'She's fucking crazy, Brian.'

'It's the tumour. We'll just have to keep a closer eye on her. There's nothing much else we can do.'

'If she buzzes, I want you to get her.'

'Okay. No problem.'

But she didn't buzz. At about five o'clock, Brian quietly unlocked her door and poked his head in. Joyce was fast asleep in bed, but twitching, just like the possum. In the morning, Brian sat in Joyce's room to give Sandra support while she monitored her showering and breakfast. Joyce had blood crusted on her but it all washed off. It was the possum's. She hadn't even been scratched. Brian was thinking how difficult it would have been to kill a wild animal like that with a knife. Maybe she killed it first somehow and then slit it open to shock them. You couldn't ask her, not least because Brian didn't want the incident revived in her mind, and in fact although Joyce complained about this and that as usual, she took her meds as instructed and made no reference to the night's event. It seemed, in fact, that she really had forgotten what she had done.

Then, as often after some highly dramatic incident, everything in the home seemed to settle down. Even Joyce was uncharacteristically docile. It was like a mild spell had been cast upon the residents, as though they were under some kind of external instruction to behave themselves after such an outrage on poor old Pete. Another of those mysterious herd phenomena, so Brian assumed. Brian and Angela made sure that all the staff kept up to the mark in terms of security measures and drug monitoring. Everybody did what they should. Only James remained a problem, and only with Angela.

'Look, I know you feel you need to deal with James, but he's only one resident. What does it really matter if you just avoid him?'

'Forget it, Brian. It matters to me.'

'It's like you're punishing yourself with him.'

Which might be true, thought Angela. James kept making references to being the Devil to provoke her, and now she was having occasional nightmares where he actually was the Devil. She always woke up from them with a sense of her own special sin, her unstoppable dirty thoughts. James was deformed on the outside, and she was deformed on the inside. She had thought only God and herself knew it, but now she was thinking James knew it too. Perhaps he had known it all along.

The two p.m. to ten p.m. shift. Brian on again with Helen. No one had commented on how he was setting the roster so as to spend time with her, although it was becoming pretty obvious. She hadn't commented on it too, which was a good sign. Was Brian fooling himself or was the warmth between them becoming more than collegial? They were sharing a quiet tea at the hub. He smiled at her through the steam. She smiled back.

'You seem very chipper today,' she said.

'I am. In fact, I've had some great news. An old mate of mine rang me a couple of nights back. He's a filmmaker and he's somehow got the finance together, grants, investors, whatever to start on a feature he's been working on and off for years. Part of the story is set down here in the wilderness and he wants me to come on board as one of the editors.'

'Congratulations. I thought you told me you were out of touch technically and so on.'

'He's going to train me up. It's full-time work for six months at least. It's a fantastic opportunity. I'm back in business, Helen.'

'What about your job here?'

'I've resigned. You're the first to know. It's the break I thought would never come along.'

'When do you go?'

'A week. This Saturday's my last shift.'

'I'll miss you, Brian.'

'Well, I'm not leaving the state.'

'No, that's true. So then we can still catch up.'

'Of course.'

'I'd like that.'

Here it was. All his Christmases were coming at once.

An impromptu farewell party for Brian was set for Saturday night. He was on with Geoff for the two p.m. to ten p.m. shift. Permanent and casual staff were invited at eight thirty, after the residents had gone to bed. Angela offered to make a non-alcoholic fruit punch, and after ten, whoever wanted could join Brian for a drink at the Republic Bar in North Hobart, where Alan often played.

Angela turned up late afternoon with all the necessary ingredients for her punch including a large bowl she'd purchased on the way from K-Mart. She compiled her concoction in the kitchen and Brian and Geoff transported it to a low coffee table placed next to the hub. Watched on by Gwen, Angela hung streamers and other bits and pieces around the hub and generally helped set up with glasses and snacks until eight thirty, when all the permanent staff turned up, plus two casuals, Sally and Ian, a couple who had met at the home and were now engaged.

Despite the lack of alcohol, by nine, all were obviously enjoying themselves. Old stories and new. Brian was touched. He had worked there for so long and now realised how much affection he had for his workmates and also some of the residents. He had said lengthy good-byes to the latter throughout the afternoon. He would miss them. They were in bed and, unusually, there were no interruptions from any of them. Angela held Brian's buzzer. Give him a break. Everyone was tucking into the punch, which seemed to have been a great success. Suddenly weary, she sat down on one of the chairs brought in from the dining room and closed her eyes.

She opened her eyes. Her throat was parched and her head throbbed and ached. Her mouth was gagged and she was tied painfully to the chair. She struggled but the knots were firm. She looked up and her eyes met James's.

'My sleeping princess, first to awake.'

Behind James was Joyce, holding a large kitchen knife. She sliced the air with it in a repeated figure-of-eight pattern as she swayed from side to side, eyes closed, humming tunelessly. Angela strained to look around. All five permanent staff from the party, plus the two casuals, were bound like her, asleep, doped on the stolen tablets. Beyond their circle, it looked as though all of the clients were out and about, many floating ethereally. It was the hour of the sundowning. She had slept all night and through the day.

James followed her thoughts. 'Don't worry. They've all been fed and watered. After a fashion. Couldn't manage the meds but that won't matter. Let me take off your gag, my dear. There, that's better.'

She gasped, trying to take it all in. She could scream the house down, but to what effect? James smiled at her complacently. What did he want?

'How did you doctor the punch?'

'Rufus did it. We'd ground up all the pills weeks back. We just needed an opportunity. This was perfect, we could get the whole lot of you. Stroke of luck. Gwen gave us the nod when at some point in the afternoon you three were away, the boys on jobs, you in the loo or somewhere. A full cup of powder. I'm surprised you didn't taste it.'

The residents didn't seem to be worried at all about Angela and the rest being bound. Particularly because, she now supposed, James had promised them their freedom.

'We'll wait for the others to come to, and then we'll begin.'

They waited a while in silence, save for Joyce's hum, but the rest of the staff remained asleep.

'Looks like I overdosed. I'm not trained like you. Still, better safe than sorry, I always say. I apologise for your missing church this morning, Angela my dear, but then you'll be pleased to know you'll be meeting your maker shortly.'

She looked up at him. Still the complacent smile. What did he mean? More mind games? The minutes ticked over. Still nobody woke.

'I think we should make a start. Joyce, the lovely Angela seems to have nothing to say. Gag her again, will you?'

Joyce tied the cleaning rag back tightly around her head.

James looked at her with his serious indrawn expression. 'I don't want to run out of time. It really only matters that you're awake. This is Joyce's idea. She wanted you all to know. I was perfectly content to let Rufus set fire to the place while you were out to it, but it does give me satisfaction for you to know, Angela. Puts a cap on the act. I need you to understand that I'm killing you particularly, not because of who you are, but what you are. But there's nothing personal here. You're a good godly person, and beautiful and whole. Killing you, I strike at God, my real foe. Who has blighted my life, and the lives of the others as well. Pure capricious malevolence. Well, I know it's only killing His messenger, but after all, that is a long and honourable tradition. Now you make sure you tell Him what I said. Joyce! It's time!'

He wasn't going to let her hack them all!

He saw the horrified look on her face. 'No, not the knife. Joyce would be up for it, certainly, but it's too disturbing for the residents.'

Joyce had moved behind the slumped figure of Brian. She had placed down the knife and was holding a long thin cord, an elastic gardening tie, Angela thought. She looped it deftly around his neck and suddenly pulled it tight, her wrists and arms straining, her head thrown back and eyes closed. James watched intently. There was no sound. Five or so minutes. Brian's feet jigged a little and then his body slumped. Joyce still held the cord taut.

'That's enough, Joyce. Next.'

And so in frozen horror Angela watched her garrotte all seven. It was relatively quick and efficient. Not clean, though. A few released their bowels. James wrinkled his nose in distaste.

Finally, it was her turn. James wheeled closer. It had come to this.

'Therefore you also must be ready, for the Son of Man is coming at an hour you do not expect.'

But she was not ready, she was still full of sin, had not had time to clear a space for herself in preparation. The cord was around her throat, and then she was choking. It was vile, unsupportable. Through her agony, Angela became aware that James had taken the tie from Joyce. She sent up a final prayer, and everything came rushing inwards.

James watched the leaping flames. Glorious they were, and from their flickering tongues the great mount of smoke and sparks billowing up against the mass of the forest and the night sky and its infinite stars. Rufus, meticulous as ever, had done an outstanding job. The codes and now this wonderful fire. All their shadows danced crazily behind. Deep deep satisfaction. Death and destruction polluting the pure mountain air. Radiant heat scalding his eyes and frost nipping at his feet. Yes, a bitter winter's night, but soon they would be on the move.

No one around would worry about the blaze. Unless it spread, the distant neighbours would just think it a backyard burn-off. Rufus and Ben were busy placing large stones across the road. Then in front of these they set down the 'No Entry' billboard constructed in the communal workshop. Yellow and black, nicely official. The way now was clear to the city.

His trusty lieutenant, mad Joyce, was manically marshalling the troops with her knife. Some had already wandered off. He'd seen Mavis Connell make a beeline into the bush. But most were here right with him, on wheelchair or foot. Bertie was chafing at the bit, pacing back and forward across the short width of the road sporting his checked racing jacket, shiny with age, and a plastic bow tie. Even Gwen had happily swapped her long-time station for freedom and revenge. They were all primed for it.

Above the ambient hum and crackle there was a roar, a blast, a flare and intense flush of heat. James looked up with the rest to watch the front of the home collapse, revealing its roasting interior like the oven of a crematorium. The hub was transfigured. The eight care workers in their various postures glowed independently as though fired from within. Then each gradually cracked open, crumbled, and their skulls and confederate bones, ribcage, pelvis, femurs, gently subsided into long shimmering mounds of ashes.

Joyce clapped her hands smartly, and they turned back towards him, expectant. It would take them a few hours. They had their weapons, kitchen and garden implements. Any house they passed en route they would torch, any individual they came across they would kill. But there was not much between here and the city, where he would wreak his havoc, vengeance, before they cut him and his troops down. He would make his mark, they would know his anger at not being whole, at being blighted, they would know, and they would remember. Angela's God would know above all.

Joyce approached him, ecstatic, wild.

'We right to go, Joyce?'

'Fuck the world! Fuck the world!'

'That's my Joyce. Everyone here? Follow me!'

James wheeled to the front of his motley crew, the former residents of the Happy Valley Nursing Home strewn across the empty macadam of Snake Gully Road, the disabled and the abandoned, God's forgotten. He threw back his head and gave an exultant cry which echoed around the hills, and in one demented accord, they all hit the road to Hobart.

Final Role

'Sandy! Sally! What are you two doing here?'

A pause, then Sandy: 'We live here, Sigrid.'

It made no sense. Sigrid had turned a corner and suddenly there was this couple who she hadn't seen for as many years as she could remember. The three of them facing off in a deserted lane flanked by light industrial buildings in Derwent Park. It was six o'clock and the workers had all gone. No cars, no people. Dust and concrete. Sally regarded her puzzled face with slight condescension. Sigrid recalled how she had always patronised her.

'We live a couple of streets away. Our evening stroll.'

'Right.' Sigrid had driven past the block. Right was wrong. She had not disguised the surprise in her voice, that these two, who when she last knew them – well-off and living in a spacious Federation cottage in salubrious Sandy Bay with their boys at Hutchins – had somehow descended to public housing in the northern suburbs.

Furthermore, they looked old. Sigrid was sixty-five, but these both looked older than her, even though they were a few years younger. Sandy particularly, she'd fancied him for a time after Jim died. Sally had known it too – one reason for the patronising – and here he was stooped and wizened, left arm in a plaster cast.

He saw her glance at it. 'Tripped getting out of bed. Onset Parkinson's.'

'That's no good.'

'So, Sigrid,' he continued, 'some hard times since last we met.' His voice was still posh.

'I'm sorry to hear it.'

'Long story short. I was made redundant at Tas. Water, like most of the middle management, and then this diagnosis. We had no health insurance and had to sell up. We're lucky to be here, matter of fact. A nice little unit, homely. Sally and I are quite comfortable.'

'And the boys?'

'Well, Richard, if you remember, moved to the mainland. We haven't heard from him in a while. John, our younger, works for a local builder.'

The only thing Sigrid remembered about Richard was Sally boasting how he had topped some maths competition. What had happened here to these once proud and prosperous folks? Life had taken them down a peg or two. Actually, life had fucked them over. Little wonder Sigrid hadn't seen them around.

'And yourself?' asked Sally with one cocked eyebrow. 'What brings you to these parts?'

'I'm looking for a pub, the Four in Hand.'

'You're not far,' said Sandy. 'Up the end of this street around to the right. Can't you hear it?'

She could now, a soft thump-thump. Also see the glow of it above a line of buildings against the darkening sky.

'Sally and I dropped in once. Too young for us.'

'I've been invited to a season launch of a new theatre company: Shout Out. A daughter of a friend at work, one of their collective, has asked me to be their patron.'

'You still tread the boards?'

'Not for years. With work these days I just haven't the time. Done a bit of mentoring.'

'You're still working.'

'Yes. Sure.'

'You were a partner at Dakin's, that right?'

'There seems to be more work than ever. Maybe I should slow down.'

'Well, it's been nice catching up,' said Sally. 'Enjoy your evening, Sigrid.'

She had already taken Sandy's arm and steered him on. Didn't want to prolong matters or suggest further meetings. Neither did Sigrid. They had all known one another so well, friends of friends. At one point, they seemed to be at every social event Jim and her attended. Now she would probably never see them again. Anyway, up the road and to the right, as directed.

A hipster pub, so one of her younger colleagues had warned her. Raffishly staking out territory in a downbeat locale. Sign of the times? Who knows, who cares? Sigrid would make her appearance, drink one beer, watch the launch and depart. The bar had taken over what appeared to be an old lumber yard. Industrial chic in spades, or disused decaying junk strewn wherever, depending upon your point of view. A few OH&S issues. She approached two young men sitting on oil drums drinking pints, both sporting flannelette shirts and trim beards. They looked up at her, blinking.

'I'm here for a theatre launch.'

'Inside, I think you'll find.'

Flannelette shirts, but the accent definitely not bogan. Back to their beers. As she weaved her way through the rubble towards a vast corrugated-iron barn, Sigrid reflected that if she had entered this yard times past, those men would have noticed her at once, surreptitiously glanced at her as she walked up to them, then openly watched her as she walked away, perhaps with comment.

She was now 'invisible', as her women friends termed it. Released from the male gaze, pluses and minuses, but she had adjusted, unlike a few of those friends.

Anyway, these days the male gaze was considered in the media et cetera somewhat 'off'. Rude and discourteous. But having once been a 'good sort' plus an actor, it was a thing Sigrid had been well accustomed to. Men were wired slightly differently, and you just needed to know how to deal with that. No longer.

She entered a high open space packed with people and noise. And more junk. She took in the crowd for a while hoping she would recognise someone. Again, times past, she could have walked into any theatrical event and know half the house. Not here, and this was, she saw, because everyone was at least was thirty years younger than her. No matter. Get a drink, find a spot and wait for whatever to happen.

'What'll it be?' The barman was drop-dead gorgeous, like a god. An aspiring thespian?

She must not stare. The old-woman gaze. Problem was, she didn't know any of the beers. 'What would you recommend?'

He proceeded to describe them as though they were courses on a menu.

'Just some kind of light lager, thanks.'

'The Honey-leather Malt?'

'Sounds good.'

She paid with her phone – see, she was as up with it as they were – then, armed with her drink, struck out for the thick of the mob, beyond which, in the bright gloom, a makeshift stage with an ornate proscenium arch constructed from even more junk loomed like a strange mirage. Amongst the immediate press were rough wooden tables with benches but all seats looked taken. There was room at the end of one bench she could fit into. She sat down gratefully. It was hot. She peeled off her jacket and folded it on her lap. Then she smiled at the curly-haired girl opposite. Under a rucked up T-shirt, she was breastfeeding an infant, its eyes closed in bliss. Sigrid looked for a moment at the dark ripe nipple. She and Jim, or rather Jim, had decided not to have children, a decision she had always regretted.

'Hi, I'm Athalia.'

'That's a theatrical name.'

'Is it?'

'It's a play by Racine.'

A quizzical look.

'You're not involved in the theatre? Not part of the launch here?'

'Oh, yes. I'm playing Shylock this year for Shout Out.'

'Great.'

'This table is the entire cast for *The Merchant*.'

She glanced around. They seemed a young cast for the play.

'Didn't they do it last year?'

'It was a big success so they've brought it back.'

'I didn't realise they had a female Shylock.'

This was a lie. This was, in fact, the reason Sigrid had not attended. Then it had been brilliantly reviewed.

'I'm Sigrid.'

'Are you Sigrid Sommers?'

'Yes, I am.'

'My dad used to take me to your performances when I was young. He was a big fan. I think he had a crush on you. I didn't understand the Shakespeare but I remember really enjoying some Oscar Wilde play.'

'*A Woman of No Importance*, probably. It was the last thing I did.'

'You're acting for Shout Out?' She almost sounded incredulous, or was Sigrid just imagining it?

'I've been invited to be a patron. So are you in anything else?'

'I'm also in *Shit*, Patricia Cornelius's play.'

'*Shit*.'

'That's right.' She smiled back at Sigrid with pursed lips at the mild obscenity.

Sigrid at least had heard of Patricia Cornelius. She tried to recall whether she'd seen any of her work. *Shit* would be awkward to promote, she imagined.

'She mostly writes about marginalised people, isn't that right? I have seen something of hers but, to be honest, I can't recall it. Except at the time I did think it was pretty powerful.'

Athalia beamed at her. 'Yeah, marginalised. Absolutely.'

'Shylock is marginalised.'

'Right!'

Okay, she had broken the ice. Athalia introduced her to the rest of the cast and they all began rattling on about the upcoming production. A tubby boy seated next to her, red-and-green snake tattoo curling up one forearm, kept jabbing at the air excitedly as he made his points. She shifted out of range.

Which, somewhat disconnectedly, provoked an observation that it had been years since she'd actually been touched by a man, discounting the professional handshake. Jim had lost interest in her years before he died. Occasionally she still recalled his body, its contours, its odours. She would probably never make love to a man again. Disquieting thought. Focus on the conversation, Sigrid. Shakespeare this, Shakespeare that.

Well, Racine might be a bridge too far but they certainly seemed to know their Bard. Familiar territory; she sipped at her beer and started to relax. Then she recognised a tall youth draped elegantly over one end of the bar chatting to a girl. But she couldn't place him. He caught her eye, smiled and gave a nod. Don't ask, give it time and it will surface.

She thought further about why she hadn't gone to *The Merchant* last year, since she made a point of seeing every local Shakespeare. One further reason was that during a recent stint in Melbourne she had experienced what she had considered to be an ideal production of the play, and was hesitant to spoil the memory of it. But, of course, there is no such thing as an ideal production and one should always seek out new interpretations. She should have given it a go. That she hadn't was a small betrayal of her principles. So she had missed a good performance of a great play.

Stephen Corrs, that's the name. Sigrid had tutored him in a role three years back as part of an Arts Tas. initiative. Benedict from *Much Ado*. Although she regularly attended shows around town, she hadn't seen him since.

Nobody was paying her any attention, so she rose with her drink, left her coat to keep the place, yes, she had her phone, and worked her way over.

'Hey, Sigrid.'

'Hello, Stephen. What are you up to these days?'

'I'm into my last year at Vic. College. Won a place there, just after my classes with you. I'm sure you pushed me over that line.'

'I'm just as sure it was your natural talent.' She recalled how good he'd been. Real potential, rare as hen's teeth. She was flattered he still valued their time together. The sessions had been strong and forthright, they'd really connected.

'So are you enjoying it all?'

'Fabulous. We're doing Chekhov and Ibsen this semester.'

'My favourites.'

'I remember.'

Stepping, without thought, from the shadows into the blazing light, the adrenalin pumping, the moment wholly yours, charged with potency, larger than life.

'Why are you back?'

'Holiday. Catch-up. Sigrid, this is my friend, Pia. She's doing the course with me. We're going to get some friends together and start a collective at the end of the year.'

'Good luck to you both. You'll need it. But it sounds a wonderful thing to do.'

'We figure we've got to make our own work.'

'You do, but hopefully not forever.'

He chatted to her about his studies: Stanislavsky, Brecht, Grotowski, Peter Brooks in Paris… Sigrid had never had any formal training, another perennial regret, even though the local roles had come readily, and also, at first, modelling work. But not the proper professional stuff, not Melbourne or Sydney. The law had proved too steady, and then too lucrative. Early on, Jim was in and out of work, so she had never really been able to chance her arm, try for the schools, brave the auditions. Regardless, Jim probably would not have liked her following that path. The pro/am scene here he could tolerate. Sport, not theatre, had been his thing. And he was tied to Hobart.

There was someone talking from a mike from the stage. The hubbub subsided. Stage lights focused the crowd. Two actors introduced themselves and then proceeded to perform an excerpt from the opening play of the season. Everyone leaned in.

What the piece was about, which took Sigrid a little while to grasp, was female cosmetic genital surgery: labiaplasty. The main protagonist, an apparently sane attractive young woman, felt she needed her labia to conform to some 'aesthetic' standard, for the men she was to meet. She was a trainee surgeon and for various reasons, opposition from her family, need for secrecy, cost, was planning to perform the procedure on herself.

Sigrid was horrified. Why would any self-respecting woman modify or, more accurately, commodify, the most individually erotic part of herself? Although Sigrid had vaguely heard about this business, for some reason she had never actually thought about it. Now she found the idea shocking and repellent. Where was this coming from? Net porn? The last time Sigrid had seen pornography was back in the seventies. That was on illegal grainy videos, where attractive but otherwise average men and women had sex in the various limited ways that you could. It had never appealed to her. Still, from her reading of the occasional article, she understood that porn now was different, both in what it showed and particularly in its availability. More than ever, it placed specific sexual pressures on women, on how they might think men expected them to look and act. That was what this play was about.

Okay, it was a critique. She got that. Still, she was disturbed. She looked around. Did these friendly fellows sitting around here so attentively possibly expect something like this of their girlfriends, their wives-to-be, the potential mothers of their children? She could not believe it. The scenario was an exaggeration – well she hoped it was – to make a brutal satiric point. It was about something being foisted upon them all, nefarious and commercial. It was tied up with advertising and film, the packaged female body, the cruel and bogus conformity. But surely, she considered, there was nothing especially new in all this. Just the extremity.

Which, on further consideration, in its way was no more extreme than the tropes Caryl Churchill had employed addressing the money-maker 'greed is good' crowd and Thatcher cheer squad back in the eighties. Plays she herself had acted in with ferocious and obscene relish.

And from the sample here before her, this was obviously well crafted, the playwright sharp and witty. Shocked? Surely, Sigrid, this is the reaction you are meant to have, why the thing was written. But still, she did not want to go and see it. It was too upsetting, too confronting. It was different to her not wanting to go and see *The Merchant*.

Or was it?

She sipped on her craft beer. Shocking, upsetting, confronting? So what? That's what real theatre is, isn't it? That's one of the reasons to go to the theatre, to shake you up and make you think. How shocking had Ibsen been in his day? And Pinter? In your heyday, Caryl Churchill. In the 90s, Sarah Kane.

She suddenly felt enormously tired.

Bows, applause, and the artistic director of Shout Out, a young man wiry and wired, introduced the upcoming season in an excited gabble – some vocal coaching definitely needed here. Sigrid glanced at her phone. Yes, time to leave. When the director was finished, she moved forward, grabbed a couple of season brochures, accosted him, introduced herself (the boy didn't have a clue who she was), exchanged a few pleasantries, then swallowed her last warm mouthful, and turned for the exit. She should say goodbye to Stephen. He was alone at the bar now.

'Stephen, I must be on my way. I wanted to wish you a last good luck.'

She wondered whether she should shake his hand, but Stephen, probably because he was slightly drunk, leant over and kissed her on the lips.

'Thanks, Sigrid, thanks for everything. Good luck to you.'

His lips were firm and dry. Masculine. She could smell his fresh male sweat and something else: him. He lost his balance straightening up and placed his right hand on her left hip.

'Sorry.'

'No problem.'

But from his touch, an incredible jolt zapped through her as though she had been struck by lightning. Through the fabric of her dress her flesh felt burnt.

'Are you all right, Sigrid?'

'I'm fine. Thanks. I must go.'

She was not fine. Not at all. It was like being drunk, but she was not drunk; she had had one beer. She needed to get possession of herself and leave at once.

She turned and made steadily for the exit, one step after another. Once she was out in the open, things seemed easier. She paused to get her bearings. The night air was biting, but she could hardly feel it. She had left her coat back in the bar. She would not return for it. The two bearded men were still on their petrol barrels. They didn't look up as she passed. Then she was in the street. Nothing except the shabby buildings. She walked away from the warm pulse of the pub around the corner and towards her car, solitary, half up on the footpath in the distance. Then she was next to it, leaning onto it for support. Was she all right to drive? In a minute. Just take a few deep breaths.

Standing there, disoriented, she had a brief dream fantasy. She was a sailor whose boat, without her knowing, had slipped its mooring and drifted offshore. She looked across the short stretch of water. In a halo of bright sun before her was a paradise: lush foliage, ripe fruits, crystal streams and beautiful wild birds carolling joy. She started to tack back, but as she approached land, fog descended and an adverse wind sprung up which steadily drove her into the unknown wastes.

Alana

As soon as Luke set eyes on her, he was instantly, angrily aware of every other male in the room. Not that too many of them, he reasoned, trying to get a hold of himself, a hold of the situation, constituted a serious threat. He cast a cursory, but well-trained, glance over the whole tricked-out faggoty lot of them, before inevitably returning to her. The guy she was chatting to was gay, but really gay, no doubt about it, so there was no hurry, he had a little time, to think, to prepare. Another sweep, a bit slower. Actually, there were a few contenders. And in one important respect he was out of his depth here, since it was a party he shouldn't even be at.

The party he should be at was way back down Davey Street at the Globe Hotel, his mate Michael's, but at some point Luke had wandered out bored and up the road and down a side street into this one. And this one was a scene, absolutely. Just look at these fuckers. So what is a scene, Luke? Tell me. It's bullshit. A collective mythology dreamed by every urban generation. Look around. Each conversation propelled by a tension, an anticipation that is never going to be fulfilled. Am I wearing the right clothes? Speaking to the right person? Saying the right things? Listening to the right music? A scene is always round the next corner. It's the next person you're going to meet, next party you're going to be asked to. None of these people are living, they're waiting, for something that's never going to arrive. Under the glossy façade, Luke knew they were just ordinary, ordinary and bored like him (well, perhaps not quite like him), but too frightened to admit it.

Keep all that in mind, Luke. Now make your move, now, while the gay guy's still holding your spot.

'Excuse me, I'm sorry.' In his haste, he had bumped into a girl, knocking her drink. 'Have I spilt any on you?'

She was thin and awkward with quick nervy movements like a bird, quite pretty, but her face was pinched, long curved nose, dark eyes, and her jet-black hair looked natural. Some immigrant's daughter and Daddy's made good, even in fucking Hobart. She seemed strung as tight as a piano wire, even more wound up than him. That helped to relax him a little.

'No, wouldn't matter anyway, it's only white. I was watching you looking over at Alana.'

That's the name. Alana. Perfect. 'Yeah. I haven't seen her in a while.'

'I bet. She's never been to Hobart before in her life. She's my best friend. The two of us have just flown down from Melbourne for this birthday party for her brother who's studying down here who I also bet you haven't seen in while.'

'No, as a matter of fact.'

'As a matter of fact, you just came in off the street.'

'How do you know?'

'I didn't know. Just guessed from the way you walked in the door and stood there checking everyone out.'

His first mistake. Always be confident. Always bullshit. Nobody knows, nobody cares.

'What's your name?'

'Luke.'

She didn't care. She was checking him out. Alana's best friend. Good contact.

A burly pasty-faced guy in an expensive suit shouldered in. Couldn't possibly be the brother. Wrong colouring.

'Excuse me, but who do you know here?' His eyes drilled into Luke. The tone was threatening. He also knew.

'Luke's an old friend of mine, George, from Melbourne Uni days, living here now. I asked him along. Forgot to mention it. Sorry.'

'No worries, Rachel.' He moved off.

'Now you know my name.'

Yeah, she was interested in him. What's more, he owed her, big time.

'Thanks.'

'Don't get into a fight or nick the objets d'art.'

'Speaking of which, whose unopened bottle of red is that beside you?'

'Why don't you open it and find out?'

'I don't have a glass.'

'Have mine.' She picked up a paper napkin from one of the tables and wiped her lipstick from the rim. She was goading him.

What the hell. In for a penny… He reached for the bottle. It was corked, which probably meant it was expensive, or foreign anyway, and there was a classy-looking opener lying beside it. Luke eased out the cork, took the glass and poured himself a full measure. Instinctively, he slipped the opener into his front jeans' pocket.

'What about yourself?'

'I'll watch you drink for a while. We've been going since four. You need to catch up.'

'Actually, I've come from another party.'

'Party crawling. Did you know anyone at that one?'

'It's at a pub down the road, the Globe. My best friend, Michael, is sort of the host.'

'Now I would never do that to Alana.'

Bullshit she wouldn't. He flicked his eyes across. She was still chatting to the fruit.

'Don't worry. She's there. Medical science should do an analysis on what goes on in a guy's brain whenever they see Alana. It must be weird having your dick connected to your eyes.'

Rachel was smart. Rachel was funny. Rachel was jealous. Rachel was drunk. He took a sniff and a goodly sip himself. Fantastic!

'Like it, huh? You know how much that stuff costs?'

'You read me like a book.'

'Not so difficult, Luke. That's your bad luck, isn't it? To tell the truth, I don't mind a bit of naivety. I've heard so much horseshit these last few hours.'

'So, Rachel, what do you do in Melbourne?'

'I'm an architect. What do you do in Hobart?'

'Work in a bottle shop and play in a rock band.'

'You're way out of your element here.'

'Who gives a shit?'

'Absolutely.'

'So what do you think of what they've done to this place?'

The house was an Italianate Victorian terrace but the entire inside had been gutted and reworked in early 60s retro-chic, spiral staircase, pop furniture, Andy Warhol photos, all very stylish but to Luke's eyes totally wrong.

Another man joined them, tall, thin, Luke felt he might have seen him somewhere before, but all these guys looked the same, slicked-back black hair, smart black suit, glossy silk tie, and an expression on their faces like they owned the fucking world. He glared at Luke. Keen on Rachel perhaps? Who cared?

'Actually, Luke, I told a little fib. I'm an architect's assistant and this is my boss, Joey.'

Another Melbournite. Hence the silk tie, probably. Anyway, now he was here, Luke could make his escape and move over onto Alana.

'Joey, Luke and I were just discussing the décor.'

'Uh, huh. What do you think, mate?'

Mate? 'Smart, well done, but I think I'd prefer it as it probably was.'

'Why?' Joey said with sudden aggression. 'I would've knocked the whole thing down. Pissy little terraces. Better to rebuild, I always say, than try and squeeze a twenty-first century lifestyle into a nineteenth-century building.'

You could tell he did always say it.

'…and this 60s stuff is so daggy.'

'Sure, but what about preservation?'

'These tired old suburbs are full of crumbling fossils, human and otherwise.'

He was rude too. Good. More excuse to leave. He looked across and saw, shit, Alana was kissing the gay guy like he wasn't gay. Not a pash, but it looked like it might have a bit of something behind it. The guy walked off. Might mean nothing. If Luke was going to do anything, he would have to do it now.

'I'll leave you two to the décor. Excuse me.' He took a deep breath and walked right over. 'You're Alana.'

'Do I know you?'

Her beauty stunned him for a moment. Mustn't lose his nerve.

'No. Luke. I've just been chatting to Rachel. We're old uni mates.'

'From Melbourne? I don't remember you. What did you do?'

What did he do? Think.

'Hi, Alana.'

'Serge. Where have you been? This is Luke.'

Serge looked real competition. Well built, suave. Had to be expected with such a girl.

'Pleased to meet you, Serge.

'Serge has just directed a show at La Mama.'

He'd heard of it. What the hell was it? That's right, an experimental theatre space in Melbourne. Was anyone here from Hobart?

'Yeah, I played there once myself. Not as an actor. In a band. Some rock theatre piece.' It was incredible bullshit. But he had to meet a guy like Serge on his own ground if he was to stand any chance. 'And I play in a band here too.' He let that sink in. 'How did it go, Serge. Good houses?'

'You can't expect it for the type of work. People can't deal with being confronted.'

'Yeah, I can't.'

Alana giggled. Strike one.

'What's your band?' she asked.

'Crown of Thorns.'

He could handle this guy. He was a cliché. Luke looked up at his arrogant close-cropped head. Jesus, they must have a fucking in-vitro production line for these shonks.

'Wow!' said Alana. 'I even think I've heard of them.'

Crap. Pissy little local band, and she didn't even live here. He had won. Serge strolled off. Suddenly, he noticed that she was slightly taller than him. Women are attracted to taller guys. Don't be stupid. You've made a good start. Relax. Build on it.

'You in town long? You could come and hear us play.'

'I haven't made up my mind. I'd love to hear you, though. Do you take it seriously?'

'What, the band? Nah. The other two guys are studying and Julie is a wannabe actress. It's just a hobby, really.'

'That's a pity.'

'So what do you do, Alana?'

'Oh, nothing much, I'm a sort of secretary.'

'Who do you work for?'

'Red Flag Publishers.'

''Are they an old revolutionary collective or something? I know you take your politics seriously in Melbourne.'

'No,' she laughed, 'a small film editing company.'

'Is that what you're interested in? Film?'

'Sort of… Yeah, I guess so. Well, that's what I thought. I mean, I'd like to do something exciting, and I feel that I've got talent and everything, but I just don't know what. My job sucks. Maybe I'll stay in Hobart for a while. Do you live around here?'

'I rent a bedsitter near the uni.'

'Where do your parents live?'

What kind of a fucking question was that? He was suddenly pissed off. He'd tell her the truth. Fuck them all.

'Well, I haven't seen my parents for about fifteen years, but I guess they're in the same place.'

'What? Why?'

'My father was, no doubt still is, a violent alcoholic, a fitter, and my mother's a non-violent alcoholic, and a bit of a tart, out in the wilds of the northern suburbs. They booted me out of the house when I was fifteen. Fgured I was old enough to earn my own keep.'

'Hey, that's really unusual. I've never met anybody like that.'

Never spoken to anyone like that more like. 'Well, there''s plenty out there.'

'You don't sound very, I don't know, working class.'

'I don't feel it.' No, actually she seemed interested. Novelty value.

'Look,' she said, 'I've just got to go to the loo, but don't go away. I'll be back.'

Sounded like she meant it. What now? Back to Rachel? Forget it. Alana. She was everything he could never get his hands on. Style, elegance, beauty. She was just so desirable in that little black party dress with her long legs and long glossy chestnut hair and innocent girlish looks. When he'd first walked into the party and had just stood in the doorway looking over at her, he could hardly stand it. He thought he'd have to go and get drunk or smash something.

He scoped the crowd. He hated these people. Hated them so much. Frequently he had fantasies where he'd come into a room like this, brandishing an automatic weapon, and waste the whole fucking lot of them. They had everything, but they were nothing, and they were just so fucking full of themselves. He didn't want to be one of them, he didn't respect them enough for that, but for some reason he did want them to respect him.

The other party, the one he'd been invited to, was really more his style, friendly, casual, and there were people there that he knew and liked, but after a while he just couldn't handle being there. He'd have to go back. But not just yet, not when he was doing well. He didn't want to talk to anyone else till Alana reappeared. He scoffed the rest of his wine and put down his glass. Rachel's glass. Standing there doing nothing, he felt very on edge and also very tired. He'd worked a night shift at the bottle shop and, truth to tell, the last time he had picked up a girl in this same state two weeks back he'd been impotent, and she had not been understanding. Failure. Sometimes he felt it was his second name. He had nothing really, nothing, just a lot of vague dreams. Like Alana. Where was she?

He wandered out the back door – he was starting to feel conspicuous – and into a narrow tiled yard that opened out onto some kind of public park. There was the guy Alana had kissed earlier, just standing there looking dopey. He was drunk probably. Luke would piss him off, get rid of him. He caught sight of Luke and looked at him like he was a fucking nobody and suddenly Luke was full of rage. He walked right up to the cunt, pulled the opener from his pocket, bent out the corkscrew and dragged it across his cheek. Blood welled from the tear. The idiot stared at him for a moment in horror. Good, let him see what real anger looks like, then, hand clasped to cheek, he scampered off into the park without a sound. Good riddance. Hadn't done anything like that in a while. He threw away the opener and returned to the party.

Alana was nowhere to be seen, but Rachel walked right up to him. Could he settle for Rachel? Yes, but not while he knew Alana was around.

'Hi, Luke.'

'Rachel. Any of that red left?'

'Maybe. I see you're putting in a bit of groundwork with Alana.'

'Give me a break. I was just chatting to her, like I was with you.'

'And the brother too.'

'That Serge is her brother?'

'No, out the back just now. I saw you talking to Alan. Alan and Alana. Pretty stupid, huh?'

'Yeah, yeah. You said it.'

My New Friend

Josh carried his Pinot onto the back deck, settling on the recliner under the frangipani. Evening, late summer: the dense heat, soft whine of mosquitoes, the cove's limpid surface occasionally pocked by a falling leaf from the big brooding gums. The light imperceptibly fading. Why die and go to heaven when you could live at Beauty Point? He didn't know about heaven, but he did know he was shortly going to die (you are never 'dying'; you are living, then you die). Maybe he would make seventy. Des had said two or three years if he was lucky. No pain as yet, the drugs flattened him out; still, he could enjoy a wine or two.

If it all got too unpleasant, he would end it, in a rational way, tell Marie and everything. His papers were in order. Could she remarry? Probably. Fifty, but she had kept her looks. These days, she endured his pill-assisted love-making with equanimity, always a generous soul. Pills for this, pills for that. So for the present there were still the pleasures of *la table*, and even a little sex.

Generous and warm, unlike Shelley, his first. Thank God he'd never had kids with Shell. Now with Marie there were his three gorgeous daughters and one new grandchild, Toby, a bubbling source of delight. Josh had enjoyed his life. It had been a success; he had made a success out of it, this verdant suburb, spacious house. Hard work – enough work for two lifetimes – but also the luck of his generation, fortunes rising with the tides of the nation and particularly its premier city. The reforms of Hawke and Keating, stewardship of Howard and Costello, burgeoning markets in Asia. How would his grandchildren fare? Such a pity to leave life's great carnival. That was his biggest regret, from a few other quibbling ones.

But any life had its ragged ends. One of them was presently on his desk, a request for financial assistance from an old schoolmate, or sort of mate. Stephen Black. Blackie. How had he found him out after all the years? In this discreet sanctuary. Mutual acquaintances? Online sleuthing? It wouldn't have been too difficult. There was no escaping these days. This was definitely one he did not have to honour, but he would. Partly because he could. But also out of some odd nagging sense of obligation which Josh could not locate. Maybe it was simply because he had done well and Blackie had not. Which couldn't have been predicted going back. Yes indeed, where would Josh Maloney have ended up had he not managed to scrape second round into Commerce/Law at Sydney Uni? Where, unexpectedly, he had found his feet. What a time. Whitlam had been elected the previous year and the whole world was changing.

Where was Blackie now? He didn't want to know. How quaint, a letter. Email too casual for this, and a reminder of their generation. Josh would make a deposit and leave it at that, ignore any future contact. Blackie was an old man, like himself. Incredible. He had been like a God. Impossible to believe that such a youth could ever grow old.

He remembered his initial sighting, first year of Maroubra Boys' High, 1967, Blackie only thirteen years old but already glowing with confidence, manliness even, surrounded by acolytes. One of the naturally gifted, tall, blond, great at footy and cricket, ball sense, fast. Bright enough to slack off and get through, even the teachers carried him. Thus he managed to remain in the A class alongside Josh drifting up the grades, although they had little to do with one another.

Until one day early in sixth year, when, totally out of the blue, Blackie approached him.

Maroubra; about the same distance south of the city as Josh was now north. A decent rising middle-class-to-wealthy suburb. Ex-state-premier Bob Carr still lived there, burnishing his Labor cred. But what a wasteland, what a dead-end it had seemed in Josh's youth, when really, its status was only down a peg or two, working and lower middle-class. It was a place, lifestyle, so settled and ordinary, Josh had felt that it would never change, could never change. On the other hand, because at the same time everything seemed so provisional, built from random incidents without meaning or purpose, he had also felt, particularly at three in the morning, that any strong wind of change, from any direction, might just blow it all away.

But while he lay awake, the nation was slumbering at the far end of the known world, boring as batshit. All life happened elsewhere, the television showed you that. Summer holidays the worst, those long dreary scorchers. Absolutely nothing to do but play the same records over, flick the same worn magazines and guiltily masturbate. While Blackie lived the life of Riley. Those girls. Even at this distance, Josh could remember the unendurable ache of desire when spotting some glorious creature hanging off Blackie's neck.

'They love it, mate, love it. You just need to know the trick.'

You'd probably need to know the girls as well. Josh had been a loner. There was no way he knew how to meet the girls. Not that they would have been interested. And although Josh had had mates in the earlier grades when he'd still played sport, by his final year there were also no boys he felt drawn to. It didn't seem to matter much. No one worried him, bullied him or anything. A state of suspended animation.

He lived in a run-down weatherboard cottage with his mum – long gone, cottage and mum. She'd had one tough life. Husband scarpered when Josh was three months. His dad remarried, moved to Perth, and Josh had never seen him, nor had wanted to. His mum was a receptionist for the local doctor and he was a latchkey kid. But she had loved him and cared for him. One way or another, she was always there. You take it for granted at the time. Only later do you realise how important it is. So he was mightily pleased to be able to return a few favours some years on. Yes, that last year of school he was totally aimless. No ambition, no earthly idea what he wanted to do. With a little self-indulgence, but not too much, he saw himself as one of life's lost souls.

Then one lunchtime he was sitting on a school bench, doing nothing, when he became aware that Blackie was next to him.

'Hello, mate. Whatcha up to?'

Josh was so stunned he didn't say anything. He didn't have to.

Blackie led off. 'Whatcha doing tonight after dinner? Wanna come for a drink?'

Josh was still under-age, just like Blackie, he supposed. Unlike Blackie, he had never been to a pub, if it was a pub Blackie was suggesting. It was: the Five-in-Hand, on the beachfront. After dinner, Josh told his mum he was off for a walk. She was glued to the telly. Mid-March, plenty of late light. Josh had changed into his one pair of stone-washed jeans and one decent casual white shirt. He looked okay, but far too young for a pub. He wandered down to the beach, a little apprehensive. What if this was some kind of joke, put-up? But what kind of joke? He reconnoitred the front of the pub until he was sure he had identified the public bar, then pushed open the heavy glass-and-wood door. He stood inside feeling like an idiot but nobody minded him. The room was full of men and smelt strongly of sweat and beer. And there was Blackie, right at home, sitting at a table with a half-drunk schooner, beckoning him over.

'Good to see you, mate. What'll it be?'

Josh had never had an alcoholic drink in his life. 'What you're having.'

'No worries, mate. Sit down. First one's on me.'

He returned with two brimming schooners. It looked like a lot of fluid to Josh. He sipped his gingerly. A slightly sour taste, but not unpleasant. He'd take his time.

'There's New and Old, mate. This is New.' Blackie knew he was an innocent.

'Anything you want me to do for you, Blackie?'

Blackie rubbed the bristles on his lantern jaw. Josh only had to shave every third day.

'Not really, mate. Just felt like a chat.'

They both attended to their beers in silence. All the men were watching a television placed on a high bench which was showing the Ashes test.

Lillee's classic speed and Thompson's wild power were demolishing the English batsman who came to the crease padded like the Michelin Man. They had no answer for the bowlers and their heads were exposed. It was only a matter of time before someone was seriously injured. Each time Tommo sent down a bouncer, the crowd and the men in the pub cheered. Cricket, the gentlemen's game. It was barbaric, macho blood sport, although Josh felt excited too, but he was not comfortable with it. He turned back to Blackie, who was not looking at the cricket, but at him.

'Watcha thinking?'

Blackie was in the first eleven.

'Do you ever bowl like that?'

'Coach won't let us. It'd fuck your back anyway.'

Then a neighbour of Josh's walked past, Mrs Bourke, threading her way through to the ladies lounge, diverting the eyes of the men, as well as Josh. She was a sexy woman, a toned brunette, skin nut-brown from the sun. At odd lucky moments, Josh used to catch her smoking and sunning herself in a bikini on a towel in her backyard, through a crack in her back fence from the disused night-soil lane their houses shared. Fodder for fantasies.

Blackie watched him watch her. 'Fancy that, do you, mate?'

'Sure.'

'I've been into that one.'

Josh didn't believe it, but thought he'd tag along. 'Uh-huh, when was that?'

'First time, surprised her in the shower. She told me to get out, but I knew she was up for it. Husband's never home. She's bored. I can go in there any time. Lives just along from you. Like to watch me with her? We can set it up somehow.'

Josh couldn't see how that was possible. He also couldn't see why Mrs Bourke would leave her front door unlocked if she was having a shower. Or how Blackie knew she was having one. If he ever wanted to watch Mrs Bourke, and of course he did, it would be by himself, not with Blackie. But it was all impossible nonsense.

'Don't bother, Blackie.'

'Suit yourself, mate. Lovely arse.'

A pretty girl, younger even than them, was suddenly standing at their table. Long long hair, short short skirt. Josh blinked up at her.

'Prue, this is a mate of mine, Josh.'

'You were meant to meet me at Joey's.'

Joey's was a snack bar at the northern end of the beach.

'Sorry, doll, lost track of time with Josh here.'

'You coming?'

'We still gotta finish our beers. Catch you later.'

She turned and walked out, obviously furious.

'Why didn't you ask her to join us?'

'That one? Nah. Catch her later. Enjoy your drink, mate.'

Without a word, they slowly drank their beers and watched the cricket.

When Josh had finished his, he felt fuzzy in the head and full in the bladder. 'Where's the toilet?'

'Need a slash? Over there, mate.'

The toilet stank of urine and perfumed crystal cakes. There was space at the urinal but no way was Josh going to stand next to a fully grown man and try to piss. He felt intimidated by all this blustering over-confident maleness. He found a cleanish cubicle, then rejoined Blackie at their table.

'Another one?' Blackie grinned.

It was Josh's shout but he couldn't handle another full beer. 'I'm sorry, I've never drunk before. Just let me get you one.'

'Naw, forget it, mate. Should be moving on. Wanna meet again?'

'Sure, if you like.'

'Will your mum let you borrow her car?'

'I don't know.' Josh had got his licence some months back, but how did Blackie know?

'She wouldn't be using it Friday night. You ask her. Tell me tomorrow.' He rose, and with his long relaxed stride, sauntered out. At the door he turned and grinned back at Josh, accompanied by a salute and wink.

With Blackie gone, Josh immediately felt out of place. After a minute, he followed him out and started home. All right, there was the car, potentially, but that still didn't explain it. Surely Blackie had mates with cars. Probably girls with cars. Well, car or no car, it was something to do Friday night. He supposed.

Surprisingly, his mother was fine about the car. She was probably desperate for him to get some kind of social life.

'Just don't drink too much.'

Josh had his own small amount of money from a job he had had for the last six weeks, Saturdays from eight to two, driving home deliveries for the local greengrocer, Constantine Poulos, Con, ten dollars a shift. He was happy not to have to borrow money from his mother any more who needed all she earned, what with living expenses and bills and rent on the house. The work was okay – Josh knew he was lucky to have it – but Con was a mountainous garlicky tyrant, not least to his long-suffering wife, Sophie, and their seven kids, particularly the second eldest, Peter, who was a bit simple and also a fairy. Peter's understated but quite obvious effeminacy drove Con into a constant rage. He would regularly take him into the storeroom, lock the door and beat him unmercifully with his belt. Presumably he'd been doing it for years but it seemed weird now the inoffensive youth was just a year or two younger than Josh. Peter didn't go to school or work, just did odd jobs around the shop. He would stare openly at certain men and occasionally at Josh too.

Josh had been surprised at his mother allowing him to have the car because, although she had a daytime job, and occupied herself, in a way, with housework and the telly at night, leaving Josh pretty much to his own devices, Josh also felt that his mother, quite naturally, was over-preoccupied with her only child. She basically had nothing in her life except him, and while she wasn't overt about it, for which he was grateful, he still felt generally stifled by her from day to day. He was always aware that she was always aware of what he was doing at any point in time. On the other hand, he didn't want her to find herself a boyfriend, because of the disruption that would cause, and also because her attention might then swing entirely away from him.

But his mother seemed to have given up on that side of life, seemed resigned to the idea that now nothing for her was ever going to change, except in respect to her son, who would one day grow up and move away and make his own life. She never complained to Josh about her work, the dull routine or difficult patients. Raised as a Catholic, she was quietly religious, attending the local church every Sunday morning, but without asking for any show of faith from Josh. Although it surfaced occasionally in odd ways. One boiling day in summer, she had uncharacteristically lost her temper at him for going to the shops without his shirt on, which she described in a high shrill voice as 'indecent'.

Now it was 'Just don't drink too much', which was fair enough. Because, yes, he'd have to watch it, driving the car. Anyway, it gave him a good excuse to lay off.

Maybe Blackie needed him as some kind of sidekick in his various enterprises, romantic and otherwise, Batman and Robin, the Lone Ranger and Tonto. Maybe it was the appeal of easy company, or no company, someone there that you didn't have to mind. Blackie could install Josh in a promising locale so he didn't look like he was on his own, then just leave him to pursue whatever came up, knowing Josh wouldn't go off anywhere like himself, perhaps return to him if things didn't work out. Sort of like a base, for beer and random conversation, a reference point.

Presumably his role or function would become clearer Friday night.

Blackie didn't want Josh to pick him up. Maybe he was embarrassed about his family. Josh didn't know anything about them except for a sister a couple of years younger at Maroubra Girls, although the father was rumoured to be an alcoholic. Blackie was at Josh's place at eight as arranged. He wore flared blue jeans and a country-style soft-leather jacket with fringes like Jon Fogarty from Creedence. His long sun-bleached hair was tied back in a loose ponytail. Josh wore the same as to the pub. He didn't own a jacket but it wasn't cold.

Then Josh hung around impatiently while Blackie chatted up his mum. Blackie wasn't interested in his mum like Mrs Bourke down the road. He was employing his charm because he could and as a matter of diplomatic policy. Josh's mum owned the car after all. Blackie brought his accent up a notch so he sounded more educated and less working class. He asked his mum what she did, though Josh had told him, and they enjoyed a long joke over some TV series that Josh had never watched. He politely refused the offer of a cup of tea, and then he and Josh went out into the night and into the car, a second-hand EJ Holden that his mother had owned for years.

'A golden oldie. You right driving this?'

'I learnt on it. Where are we going?'

'The Moving Groove down at Coogee. One block back from the beach. I'll show ya.'

The Moving Groove was a cross between a nightclub and a pub. Being underage didn't present a problem, Blackie knew the doorman, who ushered them both in without a word. There was a dance floor, presently empty, with moving coloured lights and soft rock, The Stones' Beast of Burden. Blackie obviously liked the track – the Stones were a good fit for him – and he smiled to himself and shook his ponytail. Beyond the dance floor was a long crescent bar, and out the back a lushly tropical beer garden. Blackie led Josh outside, where they claimed a trestle table. Blackie scoped the scene. Two tables away was a group of four girls. One of them looked over to Blackie and smiled.

'That's May.' Blackie didn't follow this up, but produced a silver hip flask from his jacket pocket and took a lengthy swig, head back.

Josh watched his bobbing Adam's apple.

'Want a snort ,mate?'

'What is it?'

'Scotch.'

He passed the flask over and Josh took a sip. It burnt and tightened his throat and brought tears to his eyes. He gave himself a beat, recovered, and then took another sip to show he was fine with it. This time, the fluid went down smoothly.

'They charge like the Light Brigade at the bar.'

May left her friends and came over. 'Hi, Blackie.'

'May, this is Josh. Josh, May.'

She kept her kohl-rimmed eyes on Blackie. She was petite and olive-skinned with a lustrous mane of curly black hair. Loose Indian cotton shift and very tight crimson cords.

'Watcha been up to, Blackie?' A little girl's voice, stage seductive.

'Listen, Josh, why don't you buy us all a drink. Schooner of New for me. May?'

'Bundy and Coke.'

Josh left for the bar. He ordered and while he was waiting for the drinks a girl approached him, tall and angular, with unfashionably cropped brown hair and a white livid scar down one side of her face.

'You a friend of Blackie's?'

'You know him.' This was inane.

'He usually comes with Frank. Frank the plank.' She laughed at this. 'They tag team.'

Josh didn't know what this meant. His drinks arrived, he paid and, carefully balancing the glasses, made his way back to the table. The tall girl was standing there chatting to May.

Blackie stood up. 'Bit of business, mate. Back in a tick.'

The three of them walked off to the dark reaches of the garden. Josh sipped his beer. Blackie. Maybe some of his allure could rub off onto Josh. He couldn't see how. More logically, maybe Josh might observe and learn from him. Could you learn to be glamorous? Not really. It was innate and also relied on physical gifts. But you could probably learn how not to be its obverse. Josh could never be cool, but perhaps in time he could become not uncool.

Blackie returned without the girls. He sat silently sipping his beer, seemingly irritated by something. Josh had no idea what to say to him. Blackie lived a more evolved, more complete life than Josh. He did everything that one should do in a life, cricket, girls, drinking, whereas Josh did nothing. He couldn't imagine that there was anything in his own life, or anything about himself, that Blackie would want to know. So again, why was he next to him and not some babe? What did May think looking at the two of them, the mismatch?

'That tall girl said you're usually here with a guy called Frank.'

'Frank's a fuckin' idiot. Chicks usually come in pairs. You need another guy to pick 'em up. I've picked up all these chicks already.'

So Josh wasn't a 'tag team'.

'May?'

'Picked up May from the beach. Went back to her flat…'

Blackie started to describe what he and May had done, in anatomical detail, in a strange flat non-boasting voice, while all the time looking directly at Josh. Why did he seem so serious about it? Why tell him anyway? Presumably to try and make him jealous. Josh was jealous all right, but not in any way turned on, although he knew he would be turned on later when he recalled the description and could place himself in the role of Blackie.

When Blackie had finished, May, seemingly on cue, came over and sat with them again. Josh could hardly look at her after what he had heard. But perhaps it wasn't all true. Blackie stood up.

'I'm off for a slash. You keep May company.' He strode away.

May still had her Bundy and Coke. Josh could tell she didn't want to be here with him, a dag, but would wait on for Blackie.

'You at school with Blackie?'

'Same class.'

'Watcha doin' next year?'

'I'm hoping to get into Commerce/Law.' Josh said this, but it was the first time he had thought of it.

'You're going to uni?'

'If I can. What about yourself?'

'I'm fifteen.'

Fifteen. If Blackie had had sex with her, he'd broken the law.

'You have any idea what you want to do when you leave school?'

'Nup. You're lucky having something to go for. Sounds like you're a good student.'

'I need to work more, a lot more, between now and the exams.'

'You got a few months.'

'Yeah, I guess so.'

She smiled at him. One of her top front teeth was missing. 'Good luck.'

'Thanks.'

Blackie rejoined them. While he'd been gone, the music had amped up.

'Wanna dance, Blackie?'

Blackie considered. 'Another time, doll. Josh here and I have gotta do a few things. Come on, mate, let's split.' He drained his beer.

Josh gulped down his as best he could, and followed Blackie out.

'Scored some weed from Claire. Her brother's a dealer. Let's go somewhere and have a smoke.'

Claire was presumably the tall girl. The EJ was parked just up from the nightclub. As they opened the doors, Josh noticed a stationary police car parked directly across the road and the cops looking over at them. What if, for some reason, they decided to search them and found the weed. All the implications suddenly dawned on him. Underage drinking was no big deal – the cops would have done it themselves when they were kids – but possession of marihuana, even a small amount, was a whole different ball game. They could both be in big trouble. Why didn't he think? Still, too late to do anything now, just try and act cool. Ignition, gear, indicator. As he drove past the cops, eyes steadily ahead, Josh was filled with terror that the car would turn and follow them, but it remained where it was.

'Go back to Maroubra, somewhere behind the dunes.'

Josh found an isolated spot. He knew all the places having roamed aimlessly across them for years. Blackie produced some loose-leafed papers, and the plastic cache of dope, and expertly rolled a joint. He lit it and sucked back with his eyes closed, held his breath, then slowly exhaled. The little cabin stank of it. Then he passed it to Josh. Josh had never even smoked a cigarette. Everybody smoked but his father had been a three-pack-a-day man and his mother had hated it. She never smoked.

'If you don't draw it'll go out. It's not a ciggie.'

Blackie handed him the joint. It was a dare, one he had to rise to. Josh put the thing to his lips, wet with Blackie's saliva, and sucked hard. He immediately gagged and started coughing. When he'd recovered, Blackie took back the joint, relit it, had a second drag, and passed it back to Josh.

'Try again, mate.'

Another chance. This time, Josh took it steadily and managed to avoid his first reaction. He tried to hold the smoke inside his lungs as he had observe Blackie do, but had to let it out. Still, he had gone through with it.

'Wasted on ya, mate. Doesn't matter.' Blackie took back the joint, had a third drag, then pinched it out with his fingers and put it away with the cache.

At least that was over.

'Watcha wanna do?' asked Blackie.

'I don't know. Whatever you want.'

There was a strained silence. Blackie was obviously considering something.

'Let's call it a night, mate. I'm a bit done in. Just drop me back near your place and I'll walk.'

It was only ten when Josh parked alone outside his home. His mum was still up with the telly. Josh opened all the doors of the car to get rid of the smell as best he could. He couldn't imagine what she'd think if she knew. Still, in all likelihood his mother wouldn't recognise the smell (how could she?) and just think it was some kind of cigarette. That was bad enough. He could say that Blackie smoked but he hadn't. His clothes would also smell. Not to worry. He locked the car and walked in.

'Nice night, love?' his mother called from the living room.

'Sure. I'm off to bed. I've got Con in the morning.'

His mother was still asleep when he left for work. When he returned, she didn't mention anything about a smell. He had put his clothes in the washing basket and they were out on the line. She also didn't quiz him about his night. Nothing much he could tell her anyway. Josh doubted whether Blackie would ask him again.

But he was wrong.

'Same thing, mate? Friday? Eight at your place?'

'Sure.' Nothing else was happening.

Other than this one statement Monday morning, Blackie almost studiously avoided Josh at school throughout the week. Josh tried to catch his attention or initiate conversation to no avail, and soon got the message: it was only to be an out-of-hours thing. Which was a bit strange, but then it all was a bit strange. Still, Josh understood how Blackie might be unwilling to sully his exalted male circle at school, and his position at the centre of it, with the unlikely forced inclusion of a nonentity, but then surely the same logic would apply with the babes. Apparently not. Probably the babes were less concerned with the importance of any clan status and just interested in Blackie.

Which, back at the Moving Groove the following Friday, seemed to be the case. To Josh's relief, Blackie allowed various girls to join them and Josh started to get to know them and become relaxed in their company. Still, he saw that none of them was interested in him. It was all about Blackie, who seemed, however, a little irritated by the constant attention, the crossing of bare legs, fluttering of eyelids and requests for a dance. Blackie was surfeited, or something of the sort. Lucky him, thought Josh.

Although, in relation to this last thought, Josh was a little surprised to discover an unexpected response to the girls from himself. He realised, while striving to make conversation to these desirable beings, that he had little in common with any of them, which began to make them less desirable. While getting to know them, personally, all their standard wants and worries, they gradually shed their power as fantasy objects, which was probably no bad thing. It made for easier relations and although Josh was never going to score like Blackie, he could still have a socially enjoyable, if slightly dull, evening.

May was more possessive of Blackie than the others, and at one point she and Blackie went to the back of the beer garden and had what looked like an impassioned argument. After which, Blackie informed Josh that he was going off with May, and promptly did. The remaining girls drifted away from the table and Josh finished his beer and drove home. He was not unhappy or disappointed. The novelty was still there, although he could see it would soon wear off.

Blackie remained distant at school. On Wednesday lunchtime, Josh was sitting by himself as usual and, as before, he became aware that Blackie was next to him.

'Mate, I need to ask a favour from you.'

Okay, here it was, finally, but what?

'I'm in a bit of strife with May.'

Josh didn't respond.

Blackie cleared his throat. 'Problem is, mate, I've knocked her up. She's underage, her father would kick her out if he knew, so she's gotta have an op. I've asked around a bit and found someone good. Problem is it'll cost three hundred bucks.'

It was a disaster. Three hundred dollars was a fortune. You could buy a car with it. But where did he come into it?

'You work at Con's Saturdays. Peter told me Con keeps his cash for the week in a safe behind the counter and only banks it Mondays. He says it doesn't have a combination lock but a key Con keeps in a secret place, some cookbook or something.'

It was all true, but how did Blackie know the gormless Peter?

'Listen, Josh, this is what I need you to do, for a mate, a mate in deep shit.'

'You don't want me to rob Con?' This was incredible.

'No, no nothing like that. Calm down. I just need you to watch out, and turn a blind eye. What's going to happen is this: you start at eight. Peter tells me there's never any customers then and his mum and the kids are still in bed or out the back. So, just after you clock in, before you load up the van and drive off, Peter's going to start something with Con, who'll take him to the storeroom and beat him. Peter knows where the key is. He's going to take it and leave it in a certain place close to the safe. As soon as Con disappears with Peter, I'm going to walk in and take that three hundred. When Con's not looking, Peter will put the key back in Con's spot and wipe it. All I need is for you to give me the signal and keep lookout in case someone comes into the shop or is around or something. That's all. What about it?'

What about it? Josh would be accessory to a crime. Worse than the marijuana. Although he wasn't directly implicated and could simply deny knowledge, he was elsewhere in the shop when it happened, at the back checking his deliveries, whatever. Blackie had given him an out, and that's only if Blackie was caught red-handed, because it did seem like a workable plan. Peter was no doubt infatuated with Blackie and would do anything for him. Josh didn't like being roped in like this, not one bit, but then what was the alternative? If May didn't have the abortion, both she and Blackie's lives would be ruined. May was a sweetie, an innocent in a sense. And Blackie had made a mistake. Really, it could happen to anyone.

'Come on, mate, I'm totally desperate. I can't think of any other way. If it goes wrong, I'll say you knew nothing, I swear to God. You just have to watch, that's all.'

Josh tried again to think through all the implications.

'Mate, I promise nothing will happen to you.'

'Okay, okay, I'll do it.'

'Jesus, thanks. Thanks a million. I'll make it up to you, I will.'

Blackie's relief was palpable. The only time Josh had seen him lose composure.

'So when's this going to happen?'

'This Saturday if you're up for it.'

It was all so quick. Had he just made a big mistake?

'We'll skip Friday night,' said Blackie. 'I couldn't enjoy myself.'

'Okay, Saturday.'

And that was all. Blackie didn't talk to him the rest of the week, which, considering, was a relief.

Saturday morning, nothing out of the ordinary, except Josh hadn't slept all night. He turned up to work before time with damp under-arms, greeted Con, and began sorting the deliveries, trying to focus on what he needed to do. Maybe it wouldn't happen, Blackie would get cold feet. But a few minutes later, Peter appeared and started laughing in a high whinnying tone, something that particularly irked Con, and Josh knew it was on.

'Stop it, you fucking idiot,' in his thick Greek accent, while not looking at him. His embarrassing son.

But Peter kept on. Con dropped what he was doing and started shouting at him in dialect. He quickly lost it and dragged Peter out the back. There was no one in the shop except Josh. He stepped out the front. The day was crisp and fine and the air was still. Nobody was around, nothing was happening, except Blackie was across the street. Josh nodded and Blackie quickly crossed and passed him. Josh stayed where he was.

Some minutes later, Blackie walked out without acknowledgement and trotted quickly away up the street and around a corner. That was it.

Josh returned inside, Con reappeared without Peter, and Josh got on with his day.

Except of course, that wasn't it. Monday after school, a policeman, Sergeant O'Connor, was knocking on Josh's front door. He knew his mother – the sergeant also attended her church – who invited him in and then offered him a whiskey from a bottle Josh didn't know existed. The sergeant gratefully accepted. It was the end of the day.

Well-seasoned, overweight, O'Connor proceeded to give Josh a de-tailed grilling, taking careful notes, but it was apparent to Josh that he wasn't much of a suspect. He'd had no idea where Con kept the key, Con didn't know when on Saturday or perhaps Sunday he'd been robbed, Josh had been out in the van most of the time, and the children and wife would be far more likely to be able to have done it. With the lack of anything specific, greed as motive would presumably have been the same for all, but Josh didn't have any money in case there was a search. There wasn't. When he'd finished with Josh, the sergeant had a few quite words with his mum and left.

No one was caught. At work next Saturday, Con was sullen and brooding, a smoking volcano. It had obviously been a difficult week. A new combination safe had been installed and a security guard was out front, who Con hired for a month. Josh wondered who Con suspected. Maybe his wife. No doubt he was biding his time, hoping something would come up. Still, it was a one-off, the shop was a good business and Con was relatively wealthy, so in time he seemed to take it in his stride. Of course, if he ever found out, there would be hell to pay. Josh kept on with the job. He felt guilty every time he showed up, but to quit might look suspicious. Never, ever would he do anything like that again.

That Saturday morning, post-robbery, Josh kept his head down, for much was on his mind, not least of which was the previous evening. For despite everything, Blackie had wanted to go out to the nightclub as per usual. Sitting in the beer garden sipping his drink he appeared to be back to his usual relaxed self, as though nothing had happened at all. May was absent.

'She's a bit crook, mate, but she'll be right.' He winked at Josh and that was it.

The girls clustered round, seemingly more attentive to Blackie now that their main rival was missing. Again, Blackie seemed simply irritated by them.

'You know, mate, this place is a dump. We should go to a real night-club, one in the city.'

Drug-dealing Claire laughed. 'You might get in, Blackie, but no way they'd let in Josh.'

Blackie frowned. 'They don't mind letting in the underage chicks. Hey, Josh, we could dress you up as a chick and get you in that way.'

It was a joke, obviously. Still, Josh thought it was a somewhat bizarre thing to say.

Claire also seemed out of sorts. 'Come on, girls, Blackie's not going to dance. Come on and join me on the dance floor.'

The other girls, bored, sluggishly rose to their feet and followed Claire inside to the bar. Blackie and Josh just sat there and looked out at the night. Simon and Garfunkel's 'Bridge Over Troubled Waters', the present number-one hit, came on. Blackie snorted.

'I hate this fuckin' song. I hate Simon and Garfunkel. What about you?'

'No, I really like them.'

He thought that might piss Blackie off. But instead, incredibly, Blackie took his right hand off his beer, brought it under the table and, cupping it over Josh's cock and balls, began to fondle him rhythmically through the loose stone-washed denim of his jeans. More or less in time with the ballad. Josh was stunned, and to compare serious things with less, was immediately reminded in his response of descriptions of women who seized up when sexually abused, even raped. He could not react in any way to what Blackie was doing. It was so unexpected, he did not know what to do or say. He just sat there and let him.

But what was Blackie thinking? What assumptions had he made? Was it some kind of reward? Did Josh in any way want Blackie like that? Not at all. He wanted to be like Blackie, he admired him, perhaps even idolised him, but he did not want to kiss or caress him, certainly not fuck him, whatever that might mean. Such an idea had never occurred to him. No, he wanted Blackie's self-assurance, and the easy grace that flowed from it, but for himself. If he had it, really, it didn't matter to him whether Blackie existed or not. It was cruel, and he hadn't admitted it until now. In truth, he didn't really much like him.

He thought of the girls dancing inside, their heart-shaped faces, long tanned legs and sexy bottoms, unobtainable to Josh, but quite obtainable, perversely, to this man presently groping his unresponsive groin. Josh brought them to mind and there was no doubt that they, and not this, were what he wanted. And beyond that he wanted a girlfriend, to share his young life with him, walk through the park, go to the movies. He suspected now that such a thing might not happen for years, at the very least until he came into some maturity and possession of himself, but still, his desires here and now were specific and immutable.

Blackie gave it a good go, but finally accepted the non-response, removed his hand and put it back around his beer. 'Mate, why don't you and me go somewhere in the car and do a few things.'

'What things? What do you mean?'

'You know what I mean. You and me. We'll just do a few things together.'

'I'm not interested, Blackie.'

There was a long silence.

Then, 'Listen, mate, if you don't let me have a bit of fun with you, I'll get Peter and May to say that you did the robbery. They'll say it for me, believe me. I just want to do a few things. I won't hurt you or anything.'

'What? I don't believe this!'

'They'd do anything for me, mate. You let me do what I want or you'll be sorry.'

Josh was so angry he could hardly speak. 'I'm sorry, all right! Fuck it! I've had enough.' Josh got to his feet, and without a backward glance, walked out of the bar and drove home.

Predictably, there were no repercussions, except Blackie never asked him out again or ever spoke to him. Still, he would nod companionably when passing Josh in the corridor. No hard feelings. Once, Josh caught him staring at him across the classroom. But Blackie's look, when he returned it, didn't change, no wink, nothing at all. Blackie simply turned back to his books.

Which is where Josh now decided to spend his time. With considerable self-will, he applied himself to his neglected studies. There was a lot of ground to make up, but slowly Josh overhauled the material. At the end of the year, he didn't enter the exams with any great confidence, but still, he knew that he had given himself a chance. And so it proved. One of the few in his grade to matriculate, when he got to uni, he left everything to do with the school behind him.

And Blackie? With his charisma and looks and charm, his athleticism, his prestige, he had gradually, presumably unwittingly, painted himself into a corner. Seduced, like others, by his own natural masculinity, while exercising and enjoying its power and gifts, he had somewhere along the line made an unexpected discovery. There must have been, of course, but to Josh's unknowing knowledge there had never been any poofters at their school. But then it was not a place you could come out, not at all. How could Blackie ever challenge, change, all that he seemed to be, all that he was seen to be, and all that went with it? And looking back now, Josh saw how, in his way, trapped in his glittering shell, he might have been lonelier even than Josh had been at the time.

What had happened to him? What kind of life had he led? Once, maybe fifteen years after high school, when Josh was slaving for an equity firm and climbing the greasy pole of Sydney's tough business world, he spied Blackie, looking pretty much unchanged, long hair and all, with presumably his wife and two kids. They were pointing excitedly into the David Jones Christmas window display. The wife was younger, attractive of course. He didn't approach. They seemed self-absorbed and happy.

Had it all fallen apart? Too late now to worry about it or find out. Transfer the money and forget about it. This was at the other end of a life and he had present troubles enough of his own.

About the Author

Leigh Swinbourne is a dramatist and fiction writer resident in nipaluna/Hobart. His work has been shortlisted for the Patrick White Playwrights' Award, the Varuna Award and the Tasmanian Literary Prizes. His plays have been produced locally and interstate. Six scripts are presently listed (digitally published) with Australian Plays Transform. He has published two critically acclaimed collections of short stories, *The Shark* and *Away*, and a novel, *Shadow in the Forest*. He has recently completed an Australian Society of Authors mentorship for a second novel. More on Leigh's writing can be found at www.leighswinbourne.com.au.

www.ingramcontent.com/pod-product-compliance
Lightning Source LLC
Chambersburg PA
CBHW030902200726
48289CB00003B/859